PARU

A BRAVE GIRL FROM THE HILLS

SHOBHA SUBBAIAH MONNANDA

Made with ♥ on the Notion Press Platform
www.notionpress.com

Contents

Disclaimer

This is a work of fiction. Unless otherwise indicated, all the names, characters, businesses, places, events and incidents in this book are either the product of the author's imagination or used in a fictitious manner. Any resemblance to actual persons, living or dead, or actual events is purely coincidental.

Author's Note

It was a pleasant day when only pleasant thoughts came to my mind. I had just finished a quick stroll, part of my daily grandmotherly activities when a quaint idea popped into my mind.

I thought about writing a story - one that would bring awe and help focus on progressive situations. After all, is that not what life is about?

That's when I realized that this little girl was tugging at my heartstrings, waiting to learn the wonders of the world. But I was worried that the pain in the world would end up hurting her. On the contrary, the roots of courage were firm for this tough, brave girl. For her, it was to learn life's intricacies by watching her grandmother and mother, experience life. They faced the inevitable in a jovial manner, yet stood their ground as the pillars of her family. That's brave Paru, molded by life's harsh blows. What a beautiful story it would be, to see her grow and progress!

Special thanks to my family for encouraging me. My fond gratitude to my daughter for guiding me. Thank you, my grandson, for helping me at different junctures of writing this cherished story. I thank Notion Press for publishing my work of fiction and Krishna Press for typing it out for me.

And finally, my gratitude to all my readers, for having faith in me and reading this little fictious story.

- Monnanda Shobha Subbaiah

I

A Brave Girl from the Hills

Little Paru woke up and came running to her Grandma. She was rubbing her eyes so hard that they started watering. "Grandma Grandma, Somu hit me and pushed me, Grandma. I almost fell off my bed. I was having such a nice dream. The swing I sat on took me to a garden that was so beautiful. There was a plum tree there. I was going to pluck the plums. By then, this Somu hit me. He is still sleeping. I am sure he will pluck the plums. Grandma, don't let him pluck them. I want them, Grandma." Paru was sobbing.

"Oh Paru Paru, come here. You can still sleep on my lap and go for the plums. Come, come back to your dream." Said her Grandma. Paru was happy and settled herself in her favorite bed, her Grandma's lap. Spontaneously, her thumb went into her mouth, and she sucked it so happily that one could hear the 'thop thop!'

Her Grandma settled with her prayer book, chanting the shlokas on Sri Krishna, "Jayathu Jayathu Devo Devaki Nandanoyacha..." and so on. With a start, Paru jumped out of her Grandma's lap, showing her small finger and stifling a smile. She ran towards the washroom and was about to stamp on a lizard. "Oh," she screamed and cried. "Boo oo oo," and oh no! There was a little pond under her feet! That was when Somu woke up and came down the stairs. Seeing the mess that Paru had made, Somu said, "He-he-he-shame, shame puppy shame, all the boys know your name." Paru wailed louder still, while Somu laughed more and more.

Appa came from the front yard. He was watering the brinjal plot. He was complaining, "The beans in my vegetable garden have been eaten by our neighbor's calf. All my efforts are wasted."

Grandma came limping to help Paru. She said, "My little girl, my my, the pond is too small to swim! Let's get into a bigger one." She filled the bathtub—a large bucket—and made Paru sit in it. Paru forgot about all else and splashed her hands like a duck.

Well, when Paru came back after a bath and changed, Somu reminded her, "Yet shame, shame happened!" Though Paru was angry, the freshness after her bath made her sober.

The moment she noticed the presence of her brother, she asked, "Somu, did you pluck all the plums? I wanted some too!"

Somu was surprised! "What plums? I have not even finished my bath! Where are the plums?" Grandma explained to Paru for the nth time that dreams are not the same for all.

Their mother Muthi was busy in the kitchen, making the much-loved rice bread, (votti) as they called it. Paru ate it with honey and ghee. Somu ate his votti with a fried egg. The rest ate it with a nice coconut chutney with newly churned butter from Kamu cow's milk.

As Somu left for school, Paru waved to him and said, "If you find plums, get me some too, Anna!"

Muthi's coffee was always highly appreciated by all. She boasted that she learned to make it from her mother, to which her mother-in-law, Paru's Grandma, said, "That is why it's a little too strong. We use more milk, but you in towns can't afford too much milk."

Paru immediately said that she wanted milk. While sipping her milk, she said, "Now I am going to become bigger than Somu and go to school."

After breakfast, all of them went to the garden as usual. Only Muthi was a little late, for she had to clean up the house.

Grandma had planted very nice roses. She refused to use any spray or fertilizer. She made compost with cattle manure and sprayed her garden with boiled neem water in a watering can. Her roses were robust. She would also ask her son, Machaiah, not to waste money on fertilizers. But Machaiah always used fertilizers and sprays for his vegetable plots. Machaiah was more of a modern farmer, so he used ready-made manure and sprayed his vegetable garden to avoid pests, and he never agreed to use neem juice like his mother. His vegetables were big in size but maybe not as tasty as the vegetables of his mother's plants, which grew in between her roses.

Paru would say, "Grandma, why can't you use that nice manure instead of this smelly one?" But Grandma never agreed to do so and would explain, "See, Paru, the spinach growing in between my garden tastes better than those from the vegetable plot. It's healthier."

After lunch, Amma went off to prepare snacks for tea time. Somu wanted Chakkuli today. Paru went for her afternoon siesta with Grandma, and here comes Somu, back from school. That was the routine.

II

The Jelebi Joint

Appa, Machu (Machaiah), loved to take Paru and Somu for walks now and then. Paru was now about 4 years old or more, and Somu was 8 or so. It was a sad day for Bharatha. We had lost the father of our nation, Mahatma Gandhi. Grandma was a freedom fighter. She was all in tears. Those days, they had all gone for strikes, processions, and so on. She had joined the freedom fighter's group. They all joined and burnt the British clothes, hats, boots, etc. that came from England.

Grandma had told Paru how they had all abstained from school to form a heap of clothes and set fire to them. She explained to Paru how her brothers threw their hats and shoes into the fire and said, "Bharat matha ki jai!" Somu returned from school and said, "Gandhi, the father of our nation, is no more." The picture of Gandhi at home was then decorated with roses from Grandma's garden and a jasmine garland made by Grandma. All Paru understood was 'No more'. The word. 'moru' in their Kodava language meant buttermilk. She cried as others did and asked her Grandma why there was no buttermilk! In order to stop the children from crying, Appa took them both for a walk.

They walked a mile or so. It was as if there was a gloomy spell cast over all the nooks and corners of their Madikeri, which was like a little village then. There was a lodge called Ganesh Lodge in Madikeri. Appa had taken them all to the lodge for masala dosa and coffee. Paru, or 'gundu' as she was called by her Appa, always had Jelebi there. It was called 'The Jelebi Joint' by Paru and Somu.

As the 3 moved sadly, the father told them about how bad the British were and how Gandhiji helped Bharatha to get independence, Paru, the 'gundu' was on her Appa's shoulders. When they reached near the lodge, Paru screamed and cried, saying that she was tired. She almost jumped from her father's shoulder to the ground and rolled on the street, crying, Appa, Appa, I am tired." Somu was also sad to see her so.

Along with Appa, Somu consoled her and said, "I will help you; don't cry. Where is the tiredness?" he asked, and he massaged her stomach. Appa was upset too. Suddenly, to the surprise of both, Paru got up and smiled. "Now I feel better. I want Jelebi." All of them laughed when

Appa realized that they had never crossed Ganesh Lodge without eating Jelebi. Ganesh Lodge was their 'Jelebi joint'. Paru said that the Jelebi was especially nice that day. So, she said, "Can I have one more?"

Appa packed a few for those at home and ate a special dosa with Somu. By the time they reached home, a delicious dinner was ready! Oh no, it was curd rice and pickles today, as it was a mourning day. Grandma starved and cried all the time. When Paru went to wipe her tears, Somu also came with a handkerchief. The 2 of them sat with Grandma, who told them stories about her uncles, who were freedom fighters—the way they would come home late at night after their 'Delhi Chalo' trips.

One of the uncles even joined some Satyagrahis along with Gandhi, she told them. She recollected the time when Dr. Rajendra Prasad, Kamala Devi Chattopadhyay, Sarojini Naidu, and others visited her mother's place. Grandma told them about her mother, whose husband was a doctor, and after he passed away, her mother got rid of all that was western from her house, as the freedom struggle had then reached a high pitch. She said they did away with the billiards table and the huge piano, which her husband had gotten in a shipment from England. Somu grumbled, "Why did your mother do away with it? I would have played on the piano. The billiards table: How silly!"

It was a dull day, but the bush radio with batteries spoke all the while about the funeral procession, the wreaths and garlands laid on the body of the great man. Grandma cried more and more, and the children consoled her.

Somu said, "Don't worry, Grandma, I will become like Gandhiji and serve the people." Poor little Paru had to ask her grandmother for milk 3 or 4 times. When she got it, a little curd was added to it, as it was inauspicious to have milk when someone's death was announced. But she was still hungry. So both Somu and Paru secretly had Jelebi's from their Amma and went off to sleep, hugging their Grandma.

III

Festival of Puthari at Bhagamandala

Paru's aunt stayed in Bhagamandla. Grandma's sister, who was in Parane Village, passed away at the age of 62. She was younger than Grandma, and so Paru's Grandma was very sad. Of course, Grandma went to Parane a couple of times to see her ailing sister, and she did want to stay with her for a few days when her illness became very bad. But Paru had her objections and said she would stay with her too, so, Grandma had to get back. Actually, the sick sister was getting better, and Grandma thought, with good care, she would live for at least 10 more years.

But when the call came from the Almighty, it was a heart attack that took her away. As Grandma cried, sharing her woes with Paru, she said, "Had I been there, I would never have allowed Yama to take her." "What would you have done, Grandma?" asked Paru, who was not so small now. She was to go to school the next year. She was 7 plus. Her father was not in a hurry because it would add to his routine, taking her to school, getting her back, etc. Grandma said that she was too tired that day and would tell her the reply another day.

The story-telling sessions with Grandma did not stop, even in her grief. She had to tell Paru the story of Savithri and Satyavan. Grandma told her how poor Satyavan was because his father lost his kingdom. "Then why did Princess Savitri marry him? A poor man cannot smile; he has nothing to eat. So why did she marry him? I will never marry a poor man."

Grandma said in melancholy, "Satyavan was a good man. Savitri was a very good lady. So they married." Grandma continued and told her how Satyavan's life was short and that he died when he was cutting firewood. She explained to Paru the arrival of Yama, with the noose in his hand and terrible eyes! "When Yama's noose was sent to fetch Satyavan to Yamapuri, Savithri protested." At 7, how could Paru understand how Savitri brought her husband back after fighting with Yama and defeating him? Paru immediately said, "Grandma, Savithri was alone. Now we are 3. You, me, and Somu. Somu is big. We will take a big cudgel and an axe, and cut off Yama's noose and bring back your sister. You don't cry."

Grandma cried and said that it was too late. They had already taken her to heaven, as she was a very good lady. With this grief, Grandma declared there would be no big celebration for Puthari at home that year. In kodag, Puthari is celebrated by one and all, as most people in kodag depend on paddy fields and other food products for their livelihood. So Paru's aunt, Machaiah's sister, Nanji Mayee, invited Paru's family for Puthari in her house at Bhagamandala. Of course, the Grandma of Paru did not go. Paru was all excited, but to leave Grandma to cry alone, she was not prepared. So she said she would stay back. But then, the excitement was too much to resist, and finally, Grandma was left at home with her son and daughter-in-law, who planned a simple Puthari, as Puthari had to be celebrated anyway.

At Bhagamandala, Nanji Mayee was very happy to have the children. Her house was decorated with marigold garlands with mango leaves pinned in between. Crackers were in abundance. Somu was one of the main persons, to enjoy. Paru said it was injurious to the environment. Her Grandma had told her how the cracker companies engaged little boys and girls to make them and how it hurt their eyes and caused diseases in them. She also knew that child labor was against the law.

Nanji Mayee was surprised to hear that from Paru. Paru's maturity was something else. Paru also knew tables till 5, the months in various languages. January, February in English; Paggu, Besha in Tulu; Moharam, Suffur, Rabilaval, etc., in Urdu. She knew Ashwini, Bharani, etc., and the names of the stars till the end. Seasons: Chaitra, Vaishaka, and so on. Her Grandma made her repeat it every day from an old table's book. She also knew to add 2+2 and up to 20. Grandma would teach her sums with dried beans from her Appa's garden. Nanji Mayee's son, a year older than Paru, who was in Bhagamandla School, did not know so much. They were all surprised at how much little Paru knew. She knew some stories from Panchathanthra and some stories from Bhagavatha. She sang Yare Rangana, Vara Veena, and Rama Nama. Everyone said she was a genius. But Somu said, "Oh, she doesn't even go to school. So big, but sitting at home. She is only fit to cook and serve!"

Though Paru did not burst crackers, she enjoyed the beautiful flower pots. When Bheema mama carried the Kadiru, which is the paddy, from the field and came into the house, wearing Kodava traditional Kuppiya, Paru gave him milk and washed his feet. She loved thambuttu, a preparation specially prepared on Puthari Day with mashed bananas and fried boiled rice powder. The very next day, a set of people came to Nanji Mayee's house and did Kolata. It was fun. Returning home was not a welcome thing for Paru, but for the thought of her Grandma. Paru came back with lots of news, sweets, kajjayas, and chakkulies. The coconut toffees prepared by Nanji Mayee were especially nice.

Madikeri, Paru thought, was rather dull, until Grandma started telling her the story of Pannangala Thamme, the sister of Igguthappa. Both Somu and Paru listened intently. They had a picture in their minds of the 4 brothers and a sister walking down the hills, coming to kodag. The brothers were very fond of their sister. They came all the way and rested on the bank of a river on the kodag-Kerala border. They were hungry and requested their sister to prepare some rice with the raw rice they had. She found a mud pot, put some water in it, and planted it inside some sand. It was a hot summer's day. The water boiled because of the hot sand. She put the washed rice into the boiling water, and the rice was cooked. The young girl served it on banana leaves to her fond brothers. On eating, the brothers found it insipid, as there was no salt in it. They threw it up, saying, "Look! This is how it rains in kodag." Their sister found it a wicked joke after all the trouble she had taken. So she took the stick with which she stirred the rice while cooking and hit her brothers on their backs, saying, "Look! This is how the thunder sounds when the monsoon sets in kodag."

Both Paru and Somu laughed, and Somu said, "I am afraid Paru will hit me if I irritate her." To this, Paru said, "Never, my Anna, I will never hit you."

Later, the brothers collected some betel leaves. Taking some areca nut and lime paste, they all prepared their after-lunch paan. They were chewing. Suddenly, they decided to see whose tongue was crimson-red. For that, they spat the chewed betel leaf on their palms and decided it was the sister's tongue that showed the best crimson. All the brothers threw it backward. But the sister unknowingly put it back in her mouth. At this, all the brothers laughed and said she was an outcast because she took back what she had spat out. So she was not allowed to go with them henceforth. All of them took their bows and arrows, shot, and found their places in different parts of kodag. The sister's arrow fell nearby at Pannangala. The brothers and sister settled in kodag, blessing the people of kodag at different places as Igguthappa, Palurappa, Baithurappa, and so on, and the sister at Pannangala as "Pannangala Thamme."

The story became the favorite story of Somu and Paru. In fact, Somu said it for the annual story-telling competition at school and won a prize. How proud Paru was of her brother!

Paru joined the school the next June. She was taken to the 3rd standard as she was able to take the test and pass. Thanks to her Grandma, the home tutor!

IV

Paru is now Parvathy

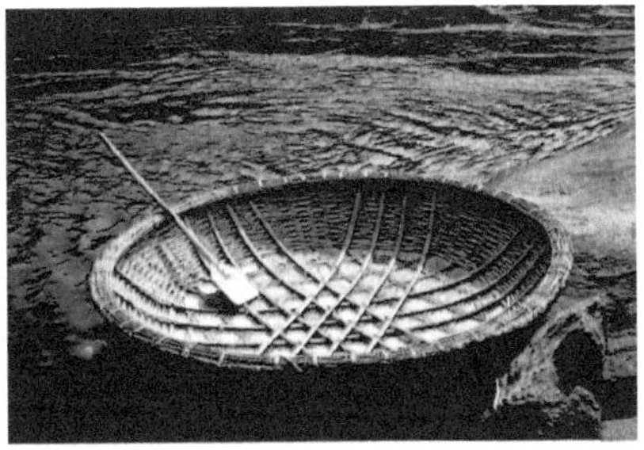

Nowadays, Paru would not answer if anyone called her Paru. She proudly said, "My name is Parvathy; my grandmother fondly calls me so because I am the favorite of Lord Shiva." Parvathy loved wading in the large pond, which was near her house. There was a coracle (Theppa) there. Often, Somu, who was now Somayya, the big boy, used the coracle and stick to go into the water in the pond. The Theppa turning round and round excited him. Since the pond wasn't deep, the parents did not worry about him. Parvathy would join him when he was in a good mood.

Often in monsoons, Parvathy's slipper would get stuck in the mire, and unable to pull it out; she would come home only with one slipper. One day, the wind was so sharp that her umbrella flew away, landing in the pond. When she went to fetch it, she got stuck in the mire. Instead of feeling scared, she found a crab and looked for more, which she brought home, and Amma made a soup out of them, on that cold day. Ever since both Parvathy and Somayya went to fetch crabs at least once a week. That is when Parvathy found the black clay with which she learned to make pots and kettles from her Grandma, which she kept for an exhibition at her school. That time, she won the second prize for craft.

Somu was now in the school final, as they called it; that was, SSLC. He was very good at mathematics. They called him Aryabhatta, as he was able to finish his exam in half the time and not one sum would go wrong. Parvathy, now in VIIIth standard, would sing and dance, and write very nice poetry. She, in spite of knowing her tables perfectly, was not so good in math, which got the comment from Somayya, "After all, she will only get married and maintain a home. How can she be clever?" That hurt her, for she knew that she was too good a housekeeper. Helping her, Amma, was her pleasure. She made very nice dosas, too. Her potato fry was very good, but she was shy about all this, for in the eyes of her brother, she was only a good cook and no good at math!

In VIII standard or third form, as it was called then, there was a selection exam before going for the boards. Somu was sure that Paru would be detained. However, she got through with good marks. Even in the board exam, a public exam, she was fifth in her class, which was very good. She was very good in fine arts and sports too. Somu laughed at her 5th rank while he secured first place in the district in SSLC. Dear Parvathy was so proud of her brother that she started ironing his clothes, polishing his shoes, and even helping the maid wash his clothes, especially the white ones. Once in a while, he would give Parvathy a hug and say, "My only lovely sister. I will always take care of you," and on those days, Parvathy would be in 7th heaven!

Now that Somayya had to go to college for his pre-university, Parvathy was quite scared to go to her school alone. Many times, Somayya would give her a lift on his bicycle!

V

Somu goes out of Town

The tenth standard, the school final, marked the end of the protected life of Somu Somayya. With very good marks in his pre-university, in which he had taken up PCMB, he told his father that he would go for his MBBS. Father was a little apprehensive, but his Grandma said that it would be blasphemous not to send a brilliant boy for a good course. Those days, a few seats were reserved for people from Kodag, and naturally, Somayya got a seat too.

Leaving home wasn't so easy for even a tough boy like Somu. His father had to tell him, "How long do you think I have to take care of you? Now you work hard, become a doctor, and take care of us." Paru sobbed like a baby until her mother told her, "Don't you want your Anna to become a doctor?" Now Parvathy said, "Oh, I do. The only thing is I like to help him. Poor Anna has to do everything on his own…. I wonder if he'll like the food there. He loved my dishes!" Now, brother laughed at her and said, "Hey! Bangalore has better restaurants Thangyavva! Do you think I'll starve? I'll be double my size when you see me next." Both laughed and laughed till the auto came to pick him up. Appa went to drop him off on the bus. Somayya was to stay in the medical college hostel. He had heard from his friends that Bangalore was a nice place with stylish people, theaters, and restaurants. So Somu went to join the ocean from the small puddle. The small fish from the tank had to face the big ones.

Traveling by a red bus was no good, but the excitement covered it all! Reaching Bangalore, his Bopi mama's (uncle's) son met him and took him home. Along with chicken roast, cheese, and bread, he was also introduced to sandwiches with sausages. After two days there, all was happy and bubbly. They even took him to Lalbagh, and they did a bit of shopping. Somu's mama, Bopi, loved him. After that, Bopi Mama took him to the college and admitted him to the college and hostel. One of his cousins was in PUC, and the other was a lawyer. So, full of confidence, Somu arrived at the college.

The welcome was good at the principal's chamber. A ranked student, after all, was an asset to the college. But when he came to the hostel, the seniors said, "We are giving you the guard of honor." They stood on 2 sides of the corridor and shouted, "Somu kee jai! Peet ko tai!" and they started hitting him on his back.

Somu was taken aback. He said, "Why is this so?"

They all said, "Oh, that is simple; it's called ragging. We got it worse. You are lucky." Then they behaved like good people and said, "He is a good chap. Leave him alone." So Somayya thought he had now won them over and went to his room.

His roommate, a docile boy by the name of Ranganath, told him, "Don't worry, it's all for fun." But Somu was surprised as to why he was beaten. When he went to college the next day, the seniors said, "Welcome, boy! You are supposed to bend your head."

Somu laughed and said, "I am a Kodava from Kodag. We never bend our heads. We are warriors!" That enraged the boys. Each one took a pair of scissors and cut Somu's beautiful hair into bad shapes. As Somu entered the classroom, all laughed at him. Handsome Somu was very upset. He just held back his tears. The lecturer entered. He asked Somu why his hair was so badly cut. Somu somehow thought it would be safer not to complain. So he said, "I had heat rashes, sir, so I had to cut my hair wherever I had rashes." The boys laughed. But the teacher said, "I admire your spirit."

The day went on. When he walked into his room in the evening, He did not realize that oil was spilled at the door. Somu slipped and had a great fall. The more he tried to stand, the more he slipped. A crowd gathered. They laughed, and Somu joined them. He started pulling down the ones close to him. One by one, many fell into the oil pool.

The planned havoc became hilarious. The intended agony became ecstasy. The group enjoyed it. but was disappointed and planned new ragging methods. The next day was different. College was normal. On his way back, Somu was asked to remove his shirt. He did so. They said, "Take off your trousers." Somu said, "Oh, here I am." Then they said, "Now, run to the college." He ran. When he came back, his bag in their care was not there.

Somu looked around. He said, "Ok, I will write again" and laughed. When he entered the room, the boys were inside the room, with food and coffee. "To greet you," they said and handed him his bag. All sat and ate. "Now pay the bill, Rs. 130," they said. Somu said I have Rs. 45. Who will give the rest? Can we go Dutch?" They all put Rs. 5 each and collected Rs. 105. So, now for the Rs. 25? Somu told the canteen guy, "Next month, brother." He agreed. The boys said, "Somayya, my boy, you have won our hearts. Any problem, tell us. Let us deal with it together." Never again was there any problem!

Now it was time for the first-year MBBS tests, preparatory exams, and special classes. The finals were around the corner. Somayya was a very good student, and his room was a tutorial for all. No one had to go for tuition. They all got free tuition! So every day, all of them ate good food, getting it from outside, as the food in the college hostel was mediocre.

His Bopi mama and family, who were ready to keep him in their house in case he found hostel life tough, were surprised to see him so happy in the college and hostel. The lawyer cousin said, "Amazing Somu, you proved you are a Kodava after all."

VI

Back Home for Kailpod

Fun-loving Somayya kept his badly cut hair as it was, just for the fun of it, and his father, who came to fetch him from the bus stand, drew his breath. Hugging him, he said, "What on earth has happened to my son? Are you alright?" and he inspected him from top to toe. He shook his head with no comments.

As he walked home, his old friends, his neighbors, the shopkeepers, the thathas (the old people), the little ones, and the new arrivals all rushed to see the budding doctor. The village so far had only one homeopath (a self-taught one) and a Nati Vaidya (village doctor). The government hospital was poorly kept. Some politicians had got it here for their mileage, and it was forgotten later. Some nurses who took leave all the time and a doctor who never came to the town of Madikeri were the only staff. So the villagers looked forward to their Somu to save them from their agony!

Photo credit: Subbaiah M Nuchimanyanda

The delay in reaching home, as he had people to talk to on the roads, was rather objectionable. Grandma was tired as she had to wait sitting on a chair. Mother was trying to finish off her work in the cow shed as the cow, Pattathi, had calved. She was also excited about the Ginnu

Pal, which is a specialty in Kodava homes when the cows had calved. Appa, forgetting all else, took him straight to the cow shed to show him his new ox, Vajra, which he had bought along with 3 acres of paddy fields near his house. That was his first investment after he retired from the army. He was a Subedar Major. When he retired, he got 2 acres as an army benefit, and he purchased another, along with an ox. So Kailupolud was special in the home of Machaiah this year.

Parvathy had stitched a cap for her brother, as her Grandma had bought a sewing machine for her. The young boy, Somayya, was happy to see everyone happy. Only he saw his mother, not so happy.

As is the custom of Kodavas, he touched the feet of all the elders and hugged his sister. Mother suddenly had tears in her eyes. Somu noticed, that the diamond earrings were replaced by small ruby ones. The 4 gold bangles were replaced by more glass ones, and his Grandma's double chain was not on her. He hugged both and said, "Avva and Grandma I will never forget your sacrifice. You both did it all for me! I will take care of you." His mother protested, "No! It's not that. These are tears of happiness."

Later, Paru told him how, day after day, the expenses rose. Their father got his land and had to spend on the land. He went to the fields and plowed his land, and today he was getting ready for Kailpod, keeping all his weapons and work material in the prayer room.

Quietly, but full of prayers, the festival was celebrated. Somu washed both his mother's cow, Pattathi, with reverence and his father's ox, Vajra, with awe. He washed and cleaned the plough and other instruments that belonged to the farm with such respect as though they were the jewels of his Avva and Grandma. The gun, he polished so well that his Appa was in tears. "My son, you shall own all this and more." Parvathy found herself planning her future. She wanted to take up teaching after her SSLC.

Luck was on their side. Just before leaving for college, Somu noticed that his grandmother limped a little more than before. "No, Grandma, not yet. Give me just 5 years. Then you are mine, and God willing, I will be here in my own nursing home!" His Grandma already saw her own dreams coming true.

VII

Today was Paru's Day

Parvathy was in her dream world. Of course, Grandma was building castles in the air. No one bothered much about Paru, as Somu was around. So she was happily sitting on her rope swing in her cow shed. The new calf was there too, with its mother. The cowherd, Samba, used to come to clean up the shed and milk the cows. The other day, the milch cow, Pattathi, kicked Paru's mother when she was milking the cow, and she fractured her toe. That was when Somu was at home. Both Somu and Paru tried and could hardly get any milk. So Samba was engaged for her mother's help. In fact, that was such a relief, as my mother was getting tired easily these days.

Samba and Somu created a swing for Paru, and that was on Paru's birthday. Mother had baked a banana cake using charcoal and sand. With Grandma's guidance, she melted sugar and made a light icing. She made Somu write "Happy Birthday, Paru" on it. Paru once again declared, "I am not Paru, I am Parvathy!" Yet, after a while, Paru remained Paru, and so did Somayya remained Somu.

Somu left for college after his holidays. Paru would swing sky-high and enjoy the fun. Now that her brother had promised to come back to the village and work as a doctor, Paru was already planning to train herself to be a nurse there! She would suddenly dream of swinging in her swing up to Anna's college and helping him fold his clothes. In her dream, she would often fall and suddenly wake up and go to her Grandma's room. Grandma once said, "What will you do once you are married?"

Paru would blush and say, 'Whatever you did, Grandma and both of them would laugh'. She would sometimes dream of being Seetha and would swear that she would never leave her home like Seetha, allowing her father-in-law to die and the mother-in-law to grieve. She would think that when the family stood in harmony, together no power could ever defeat them.

Going to college was not possible as Anna's education was of top priority. But whenever Somu said, "Don't worry, we will get you married to an affluent boy," Paru felt belittled. She knew marriage took away liberties.

She had to do some of her mother's jobs nowadays, as her mother would grow tired easily. When the 'Asha' nurse came and checked, they realized it was diabetes that made her so weak. Grandma laughed at her and said, "Keeping me healthy, you lost your health." In reality, she had lots to worry about. Loans were taken to educate Somu, and that was not mentioned to anyone. Appa was also worried all the time. Paru would help him in his fields, where he now had to engage some laborers. It was certain that, after a year or two, the yield would solve problems. But what if Paru got engaged? Among Kodavas, there was no question of dowry; thank God. But the money would be needed for a little bit of jewelry, some sarees, wedding expenses, etc.

In this regard, Mother went to see her brother, who was very nice to her. He said that he had a boy in view who would suit the situation.

VIII
Parvathy: Is she Ready?

Photo credit: Mrs Mookachanda Sitara Devayya
(Thamane Karthachira)

That was a million-dollar question indeed. An aging Grandma, a strained father, a mother slowly bending with the weight of life's challenges, and a brother just getting to settle down. Parvathy felt she had to shoulder all the burden. And now the subject of marriage! "Oh, no, Grandma! Are you crazy? Who will take care of you? Mother will neglect her health! Appa will be overstrained. Anna will have no time for his profession. Marriage, it seems, marriage. Let it be pushed to the side for five more years. I am serious, Grandma!"

Her grandmother, though she knew that all that she said was true, also knew that Paru's life could not be neglected for the sake of others.

With this excuse, Muthi, Paru's mother, went to visit her brother Ganapathy. She asked him if he could think of a good boy for Paru. After a lot of discussions, they thought Dechu, Ganapathi's wife's brother would suit Paru. Mother's brother, Ganapathy, came home to leave his sister Muthi home. It was ages since he had come to their house. He was a busy man, with his two children studying in private English-medium schools and his wife a bossy club-going lady. Though he had 40 acres of coffee plantations and some good paddy fields, he had not bothered about his sister's life. His other sister was very pretty, and she had married a good and comfortable man. Though he drank and troubled her, there was no dearth for money. Ganapathi, Muthi's brother, had contacts with that sister, as she was also in South Coorg like him. Her husband had served in the army and retired.

Gappu's arrival was very welcome at his elder sister Muthi's house. During their conversation, he told Paru's father, Machaiah, "Bava, Paru has grown beautifully. I never thought she was so grown up. What if she is given to a good boy in South Coorg?"

Machaiah was taken aback. He did not know that his wife's visit to her brother's place meant this. He said, "Well, Gappu, I never thought my girl was so big. She is such a part of our family that I can't think of this house without her!"

At this time, Grandma intervened. "What are you saying, son? Everything has to happen at the right time. There is a time and a place for everything. Let me know more about the boy you are speaking about. Is he nice to look at? Is he capable of taking care of my Paru?"

"Oh, Mayee, he is my wife Dechu's brother. He is in Dubai, earning well. Of course, he is good-looking. Or else I would not suggest him for Paru. Paru will have a comfortable life. His brother takes care of his estate, and he, Dhanu, is in Dubai. He is a contractor, a moneyed man. Marriage can be Dampathi Muhurtha, expenses shared by the two parties."

Grandma said, "Let me speak to Paru, and my Somu should approve of him, is it not?" At this, Machaiah had a good laugh. He said the usual saying of Kodavas: "Is masala ground for chicken curry after consulting the hen? Kolina ketethe masale arepada?"

All had a hearty laugh. Paru, who was listening and preparing lunch with her mom, came out and said, "Mama, are you or are you not not discussing my marriage? Please, mama, our home front is not ready for this. My mother isn't too well. Didn't she tell you? Appa is overburdened with responsibilities. We have some loans to repay. Marriage means further expense. Let us wait for a couple of years." Her mama, Gappu, laughed heartily. "You little girl, have you realized that you are no longer a kid? It now becomes our responsibility to settle you down. Delay is dangerous. Now, now, no tears. I did not come to make you cry, my pretty Paru. I shall help you in every way. You are not going out of the family. It's only your Dechu mami's brother." Paru could not decide, and nobody asked her opinion! They only had to wait for Somu's opinion. And in two days, that was got over the phone. Machu called from a local booth and told him the news. He jumped at it and said, "If he is handsome, comfortable, and well placed in life, what more do we want for our lovely Paru?".

Things moved very fast. The boy, Devaiah, or Dhanu, as he was called, came from Dubai, saw Paru, and said he liked her. But he wasn't too sure of the poor family from which she came. But his mother, Gappu's mother-in-law, who had two sons and a daughter named Dechu, said, "A girl from a modest house will be an asset to the house she enters. A rich daughter-in-law, will only split the family." As the families were already related, the marriage was fixed in no time.

So, Paru's wedding was very well celebrated with Gappu Mama's help. Dechu mami was very happy. She and her husband took on all the financial responsibilities, so the wedding wasn't a strain on Grandma's family. Somu, having taken his last exam, now was to join for his training under Dr. Raghavan, a good surgeon in Bangalore. Being a rank holder all through, it wasn't difficult for his uncle, (Machaiah's brother), Belliappa, to fix him up at all!

Grandma, mother, and father were all in tears, along with Paru. It was hell of a time for Paru's Cheriava (Belliappa's wife) to console them.

Bangalore-Baliappa and his children had a good laugh, saying, "Why!? Paru was not keen. You forced her, and now you cry, Avva! Don't cry." You always said, "Karumbena mane boru mane, the sorrowing house is always in grief." Though they were all happy to have found a suitable husband for Paru, it was difficult to bid farewell to her. They thanked the Lord and their Guru Karanas for their grace.

When the couple came for the first visit to Paru's parent's house, for mane motto, as it is called in Kodava custom, they had arranged for a Sathya Narayana pooja in the central sitting room, the Nellakki Nadu bade of the Kodava house of Machaiah.

After the pooja early that day, a simple breakfast was served. A late lunch was served with non-vegetarian food. Chicken curry and noolputtu, with bellaneer (jaggery water) for Grandma, a Naikul (ghee rice) with pork curry and chutneys, and a khuskhus (poppy seed) kheer. All the items were well enjoyed by the son-in-law, Dhanu, and he said, "Very tasty, grandmother. Your cooking is too good. Hope Parvathy is well trained!" The proud Grandma assured him and said, "My Paru is better than I am. I'll see you filled up next time, my young son-in-law." At which Somu said, "Oh, have you married a wife or a cook, my dear Dhanu Bava?" That discussion ended with dry smiles on all faces.

That night, they were supposed to stay in Paru's Thamane. But Dhanu was very uncomfortable and complaining of a stomach ache; he said he would be getting back. He called his father and asked him to send a taxi. It was a sad thing, and Grandma had so much to tell her little Paru. So Dhanu said, OK, you can stay back if you want. But except Somu, no one was prepared for that, as the role of a wife was to serve her husband!

Mother spoke a few kind words to her Paru, mainly to stop herself from crying. Grandma told her a few lines from Kalidasa's Shakunthala, as written by Adi Kavi of the Kodavas Appachakavi. "To be kind to her father-in-law, obedient to her mother-in-law, civil to her brother-in-law, to adjust with her sister-in-law, to be friendly with her husband's sister, and to be the right hand of her husband, come what may." Brother Somu took her aside and said, "Look, Paru, you are my sister. I am with you through thick and thin. I wish you all the best. Do not stick to the kitchen all the while. I am sorry that, with our means, you could not be educated further, in spite of good marks. Once I start flourishing, my fond sister, at any age, you are going to study ahead. In fact, I'll speak to my fond Bava to help you pursue your studies." Paru was happy with her brother's concern, and now she knew how much he loved her. But he had never shown those feelings! Why? Oh why?

When she left with her husband, she was more confident this time, as she now knew that she was not alone!

The newly married couple left that night soon after dinner. Dinner was simple, as Dhanu had said he was not well. Yet Grandma's rice otti, cooked on burning cinders and served with (mudre kanni) gram broth and pumpkin curry, made the grandson-in-law overeat, which made everyone happy. A peg or 2 of whisky brought by Machu's Bangalore brother did the trick. Passingly, he said, if only the house was bigger, we could have stayed! When wine is in, wit is out, and what he said was true. Everyone understood! Except Somu, who swore that he would surpass his brother-in-law at least to stand by his sister. After Paru and her husband left, a sad cloud engulfed the home of Thamane of Paru, Machaiah's house. Grandma said, to cheer everyone, "Wait till Somu; our doctor comes in a year's time!"

Well, that was that. Devaiah Dhanu was to leave for Dubai in fifteen days. He said since there were a lot of visits to be made, he may not see them again this time. Paru sobbed at this. As usual, bidding farewell, however well borne with patience, is a very painful and sad thing in a girl's life, especially when the girl is to go far away.

Yet Somu's presence filled the gap. The family rallied around him, preparing meals and hearing news of his college life regarding his trials and tribulations, which he never had time to share with his folks due to his short vacations. His holidays used to be shortened because he used to use most of them to stay in Bangalore, giving tuition in order to take some more courses that would strengthen his foundation.

All these details were not shared with the home folks. Baliappa was a great help in all of Somu's ventures. He thought that these things would upset his brother's family. Paru knew a little and knew that her brother would one day be an asset to the family. Born and brought up in a modest family, he knew he had some bonds and responsibilities.

Now was the time for him to share all these experiences. Grandma was so proud of her Somu that she already pictured her daughter-in-law wearing good sarees, getting her bangles and chain back, and walking beautifully like Paru! She never thought of herself. She knew that her daughter-in-law was a silent sufferer. They would have arguments only regarding each other's carelessness towards their own health.

One day, a few days before Somu was to leave for Bangalore, he said he had a surprise for his father. He requested his mother make some pepper chicken and burnt pork. Father and son settled at the Imara (the wooden seat in the open verandah of a Kodava house). Somu brought a bottle of whisky (of a good brand, as advised by his lawyer cousin). Both ate and drank heartily while Grandma and mother Muthi sipped piping hot, strong Coorg coffee.

That was when the cat was out of the bag. Somu told them how he worked day and night, gave tuition at a night college while he was studying, and took other classes. "All these I could do only because of Baliappa and my cousin Babanna. They always sent me back to the hostel because they believed that only hard work and a tough life could generate luck." He also told them that his passing out of college was so beautiful. His Baliappa and Babanna filled the gap of the absence of his parents and Grandma, who could not attend the same, that being the time of Okki Panni (paddy) season. He told them how much he missed his lovely family. At this point, his father said that his portion of family property in the village, about 5 acres, he would give away to his brother. Of course, all were happy to say 'yes' to this.

This time when Somu left for Bangalore, Grandma decided to go with him and stay with her elder son (Balliappa of Somu), who was her stepson, but in fact, who did a lot for her son and grandson.

Before going, Somu told them that it would be a while before he took leave again, as he would be applying for his job here and there. Grandma then said, "What about your promise to your place that you would start a nursing home?" Somu said that he had not forgotten, but then he had to earn to fulfill his dreams. "It will take a while—in fact, a long while. But remember and be firm, Grandma; you will be strong and wait for me. Do not let my mother lose her heart. You taught me to be tough and positive. You told me the stories of Achu Nayaka and (Pade Beeras) Kodava Generals; now you will be positive and help me to achieve my goal—no Grandma, your goal!"

The night ran on, and when they sat down for dinner, it was past 10 o'clock, which was never the way. By 7 PM alone, they had all sat for this break, and at 10 PM, after a good meal only with rice, beans, curry, and chicken fry (left over), they retired most unwillingly.

Machaya, a very soft-spoken man, spoke a lot that night and was very romantic with his wife, which made everyone happy. The foreign whisky did it all!

That night, Machaya told his wife, "If only I knew sons and daughters were so good, I would have had 4 sons and

4 daughters; why not now? my beautiful wife?"

"This is too much," she said shyly, and both snored away to glory, only to wake up when Mavi (avva) called out for coffee!

IX

April Fool

Somu was still sleeping. Grandma called out, "Somu, wake up; Paru is here." Somu jumped from his bed and ran out, only to be disappointed and told his Grandma that was too hurtful a joke! All laughed, and Grandma said, "Ah, for the naughty pranks you have played on me, this is nothing." She reminded him of the times when he wrapped stones in sweet wrappers and offered them to her, saying he gave them because he came first in the class. "Somu, remember once it was so soft and you had wrapped a snail in it and, unknowingly, I chewed it, and realizing the practical joke. I ran to hit you when you pushed a stool in my way and made me fall. My poor darling Parvathy massaged my back and made me recover. Is this joke as bad as that?"

Later, the quiet mother made some juice and offered it to all, and she said that thereafter everything had to be disciplined and that she would say "one, two, and three" and all should sip together, and the one who finished first would get a gift from her. She said, "One, two, three," and they all started sipping, and they all screamed, "Oh, you—you, you only behave sweet and soft-spoken. You dare serve us bitter gourd juice!" Only later did Somu realize it was the first of April.

Soon, a letter arrived from Bangalore. Somu had to go the very next day. All were very sad and said, "Our trip to Igguthappa stands canceled, as we planned it for tomorrow." Who ever knew that Machu was up to no good? He bribed the postman to deliver a false letter, and that was 'April Fool' too!

Finally, Somu declared that those at home were worse than the bullies at his college. Somu was happy that things took a different mood, and all were not crying after Paru left. Now they all got ready for their trip- a rare trip to Igguthappa!

X

Igguthappa

One of the main deities to whom a Kodava prays is Igguthappa. For rain, he is the suprema. The story goes that he and his brothers came from Kerala with their sister and stayed in different parts of Kodag to help the Kodavas prosper. Did Somu not know the story which fetched him prizes in his school?

The bus from Madikeri was at 6 a.m. So the Machaya folks, under the leadership of Grandma, started off after bathing at 5 AM to the bus stand. Each one carried a bag, one with coconuts, one with rice, one with jaggery, and the other with flowers. The flower bag was with Grandma. She tried to walk the fastest. Mother with jaggery lagged behind. Appa and his son, with the other 2 bags, pretended to walk slower than Grandma, only to give her the happiness of flaunting her health. Mother could hardly walk. Hearing the groans of his mother, soon Somu took the jaggery bag from his mother. Machu seized the opportunity and, with the excuse of helping her walk, gave her a hug now and then. Grandma and grandson kept giving passing glances and had a good time watching the Romeo and Juliet couple.

When Somu mentioned the names, Grandma wanted him to tell her the story. Our brilliant Somu had, in his college days, acted the role of Romeo. So when he told her the story, he repeated the words from Shakespeare, and his Grandma was so happy.

Another nice thing happened that day. Machayya saw one of his friends at the bus stop. He was trying to get some passengers for his van, which was going to the Igguthappa festival. He told Machu that it only cost one and a half times the bus rate. So, happily, the family got into the van. Grandma and grandson were in one seat, and the merry couple were in the other. Oh, what fun it was to continue the story of Romeo and Juliet! He hugged his Grandma now and then. At the end of the story, Grandma asks, "You, our handsome Romeo, don't tell us you have a Juliet in Bangalore!" He said that he would never do such a thing to deprive his Grandma of selecting a top-class bride for him. "Is this also part of April Fool?" said his Grandma with a mischievous look at the back seat where Machu and his Juliet were sitting.

The journey was pleasant. At Igguthappa, a surprise awaited them. A taxi arrived, from which emerged Parvathy, her husband, her in-laws, and the rest of the family. That was indeed a pleasant surprise. Pooja took place, and a thula bhara (a ritual where a person sits on one side of a large balance and rice, coconut, or jaggery are balanced on the other side) of Somu had been arranged. That was with rice, and as the ritual was going on, all started bullying Somu, as he weighed not less than 64 kg with his large, tall frame. The family, along with Paru, appreciated his maintenance of health and happily gave him the rice needed for the same.

Paru's family also had some Mahapooja, and they were all happy to meet each other again. Devaiah was very happy to be with Somaiah, and they had lots to share. So mother and grandmother were with Paru. Paru's Mavi, though a little reserved, was cordial and was more with her daughter and family. Machu was all over, and so was Paru's Mava.

All said Paru looked so beautiful with her Kokke Thathi, Jomale, Pathak, and the beautiful Pavala male given to her by her Grandma. She looked beautiful in a light blue saree, presented to her by her mother-in-law. When Grandma said she looked beautiful, her mother-in-law (Mayee) said, "Then what do you think of my handsome son's wife? Will we get anybody less beautiful for him?"

Parvathy blushed an apple pink! Oh, how lovely she looked, as Puthangarthi, as we call the new bride!

After a sumptuous meal at the temple, rice and sambar with chutney and payasam (a sweet made of rice, jaggery, and coconut) the group disbursed.

They all enjoyed the beautiful dance of the Brahmin, who danced to the beat of the drum with the Lord's thadambu on his head. That year, the thadambu (the seat of the deity's statue) was made by one of Machu's friends, and that was also, happy news to share.

The journey back was eventless, each to his own home. As usual, Swamy Igguthappa poured down his bounty in the form of rain. Reaching home, Somu was quick to help his mother with the cutting of vegetables and washing the rice. At home, all were surprised at how he learned all that, and Somu said, "Necessity is the bed of learning. I had to learn if I wanted to eat. Canteen food was insipid. So Baliavva gave me a small cooker, a stove, and a vessel or two. I ate my food, cooking it in my room. I ate an egg every day as Baliappa insisted on it."

"That we can see, my dear son! Thank God we had enough rice for the balance!" said Machu. They all laughed, but Grandma took some onion peel, dry chilly, and mustard in her left hand and took his dristhti to drive off the evil eyes and threw it out of the house, saying, "May there be good health in this house now and forever."

The next day was a rest day. The very next day, Somu left early in the morning with the bag with which he had come. Grandma had changed her mind and decided not to go with Somu. Of course, Ma and Grandma packed some chakkulis and kajjayas along with a pack of lime pickles and chandige (a rice preparation for deep frying). They had much more to give him. But how could he carry so much? They were happy to look forward to the doctor's arrival soon. Time would just fly, and their son would soon come home.

His going was sad, but all had decided not to shed tears lest his mission be disturbed. They watched him till the end of the road until he waved with his bag and wished them heartily.

That was a fulfilling holiday, indeed, a wedding over and some time spent together. All could start their chores again for the year.

XI

Parvathy's Place

The family of Paru was invited by Paru's people, as is the custom with Kodava. That was a brief lunch, as Devaiah was to leave in two more days. They were so busy visiting people that they were all tired.

Finally, on the eve of his departure, Paru came to know that her husband would be going alone, and she could go only after she got her visa! That was a shock for Paru. She and all her family did have doubts as to how she could go without a passport. But they thought that the arrangements were made by Devaiah. This came as a shock to Parvathy's family, who came to know of it only after 5 weeks when Machaiah's friend in Gonikoppa met him in town one day. After the family came to know, they thought it would be for a short while and waited.

Unfortunately, that was not so. After Dhanu's sister left, Paru was to help her mother-in-law. Well, this efficient girl happily did a lot of things. Washing, cleaning, helping with cooking, and so on. She was happy to help and tried her skill even in cooking new dishes, making her in-laws and husband very happy. When she realized that she was to stay back, a couple of tears did escape her eyelids. Yet she knew it was only until she got her passport. So she kept all her papers ready for her passport and visa. Being a good housekeeper, work was not a problem for Paru. She waited for things to happen.

Dhanu called up in a few days. He spoke to his mother and father and did say hello to Paru, whom he called "Parvathy," like he did not know her well. He told her to be helpful to his mother and not to let her do any work. Paru tried to say something—at least a word—about her passport, but the phone got cut. On the next call after a week, the same thing happened. She asked her mother-in-law, "Mayee, when do we go to get my passport?" Mother-in-law said that now it was too busy a time, and so after the busy season it could be done.

One day after her rigorous routine, which she did not mind at all, she sat with her storybook as usual. As she was reading, she heard the arrival of the neighbor. Her mother-in-law called her to make some coffee. She prepared nice coffee and served it to the guests, her Mayee, and Mava too. As she left the room, she heard the guest appreciating her coffee, so she stood there for a while, listening to her praises. She was very happy, but her father-in-law laughed and said, "Then what do you think of our choice, uncle? That is why we opted to get a girl from a modest family. We had so many people with dowries wanting to marry our Dhanu. But what will we benefit? Dhanu is quite comfortable there. My wife is getting tired of working day in and day out. I have a manager to take care of the estate. My younger son takes care, too. But with his club and social obligations, he hardly has time. The maid comes and cleans up, and the cowherd takes care of the cattle. But cooking, only my wife has to do. Now my Paru is well trained by her grandmother, and that's why we opted for this alliance."

Paru could not stay there any longer. She thought the earth had split and engulfed her. "Is this my fate? So, they have got a cook now. Oh my God, why did I not visualize this?" She had no tears to shed. She, the bold Paru of her Grandma, made up her mind to face all ordeals.

In a couple of days, her father arrived to see Paru. Paru behaved very normally. In fact, even in her in-law's place, she behaved like she never knew their plans. When her father inquired about Dhanu, she said, "He is fine. Keeps calling often. He is arranging for my passport soon." After tea and a few hours of going around the house, her father bade goodbye to her, and she was fully confident that he did not suspect any foul play.

When after a month, a letter came from Somu to his father in which he inquired about his sister. He was shocked to hear that Paru was still in India. He called from a booth and requested the telephone exchange people tell his father to be at the telephone office the next day by 7 AM. Father was worried about what had happened. As the exchange was not far away, Grandma went with him. Somu expressed his anguish as to why Paru had not gone. Father told him about the passport. When he heard that Paru was happy with her in-laws, he left the topic at this. After speaking to his Grandma, he kept the phone.

Machayya had not revealed at home that Paru had not gone to Dubai. Grandma kept quiet till she reached home. Now she took her son to task. "Machu, you did know that Paru did not go to Dubai?"
"I just came to know avva."
"When did you get to know?" she said.
"Just when I went there," he said.
"What did you say? Did you go there? When did you go?" she asked.
He said, "I had some work in Gonikoppa and I had gone there. Thought of peeping in at my samandis".
"So you went there, saw Paru, came back, and did not tell us, and why so? Do you think I am a baby? Who are you telling lies to? My Machu, who has never had anything to hide from his avva, now has reached this level. Now look here, my girl Muthi, look at what's becoming of our family! Secrets, hiding from each other. Are we all living separate lives? Is there no unity in this Kodava Okka? (house) Is this what we learned from our ancestors and Karanas?". Hearing the row Muthi, Machaiah's wife came running. She almost had a fall at the doorstep, Kattole.
"What happened Mayee? What is the row about?" she said.
"Oh you both are in league to fool me, are you? Well well,

that's the fate of those who live too long. Can't Lord Yama pick me up as his next guest? what good is my life if I am to be treated like an outsider?" she wailed.

Muthi, her daughter-in-law was shocked and asked her what she was talking about. When she came to know all that had happened, she sobbed and cried, cursing her fate. Machu had to tell her it was only because she had to get her passport and visa which always took a long time.

Anyway, Grandma wasn't convinced at all. But what could she do? She made a vow to Kaveramme that she would go to Kavery for the next Kavery Sankramana and have a kumkumarchana done in the name of her Parvathy. That night, she recollected the way Paru learned many things from her. Cooking, washing, needlework, cleaning, caring for the plants and so on and so forth. She just told herself, 'Our expectations are just a tuppence before the Lord's designs. Now only Kaveramme should help us.'

A month after Devaiah left, Parvathy realized that she was pregnant. She knew a little here and there, some by reading and some from her Grandma, and was a little upset. Then she told herself once again "I shall face it. After all, work is not too much. Mava and Mavi are nice to me. I hardly see my brother-in-law. I have to accept my lot." She resigned herself to the situation and did her chores without complaining.

Paru read a lot. Her father-in-law had a small library. There were some good magazines that came to the house. The newspaper was here after her father-in-law was done. Mother-in-law never read. She spent her time watching

TV all the while. They had a phone and that kept her busy with her friends. She would go to the Mahila Samaj and come back with a lot of gossip. Paru, whether interested or not, gave her a patient hearing and kept life going. Paru's policy was, "Anyway, I was not for marriage. What if I am here? Let me be useful and not be a burden on earth. One day God will show me the way." She never again asked her father-in-law regarding her passport. This actually kept the family happy.

One day she asked her father-in-law if she could get some wool to knit sweaters. He brought her the same and she knitted a pair of booties and a small sweater for the new arrival. It was only two months. She knew it was too early. But having nothing better to do and being a busy girl she loved doing it.

Her mother-in-law was pleased. Then she asked her if something was going on. Paru told her the truth and also jokingly said, "My husband left me with a promise! He did not keep it. Now I am so happy with you that I don't even want to go to Dubai. Maybe one day I will."

As luck would have it, that weekend, her father and mother gave her an unexpected visit. They were very surprised to see that their daughter was so happy. Actually, was she happy? Her Grandma had taught her to be happy, come what may! She made heaven out of hell. That was Paru. They arrived at 11 a.m., and her Mavi was getting Paru to make some Chikelundes (a preparation with popped rice, jaggery, coconut, gingili, and cardamom). As the last set went into the frying pan, Paru's parents came. Her mother-in-law told Paru not to tell her parents about her grief, if any. "A good daughter-in-law will only show the greener side of her husband's house, which can bring happiness to all." Paru had already decided so. So she came happily and greeted them.

When her mother-in-law told them of her pregnancy, they were happy but sad that she was not with her husband, to which Paru said, "Why? It would be hell to stay in Dubai. Imagine Me being there and no one to speak to, when my husband is out at work! I am lucky that I am here. Amma, I have made a sweater for my baby." She brought the knitted sweater and booties and showed them to her mother. She said, "My Mava brought the wool for me." It was pink in color. So, her mother said, "Why, pink, you should have a baby boy!" Paru said, "Oh, no. I want a beautiful girl like my mother-in-law. She is so smart; she goes to the club and has a lot of friends, unlike me, who sits at home reading all the time." Her mother-in-law was very happy, not knowing it was a jibe. In fact, Paru conveyed the message to her parents in her own way.

Happy and unhappy, her parents got up to leave. Mother-in-law said, "Why don't you have your lunch and go?" Paru said, "No need. Go back to my Grandma. Tell her I am very happy. I am following whatever she has advised me." She touched their feet and allowed them to go, for she did not want them to eat here. That was how she conveyed her message.

Of course, her parents read between the lines! They knew everything at a glance. They only hoped she would not be taxed.

Going home, not having the courage to keep anything a secret, they told Grandma all the news and had a very late lunch, almost at 4 o'clock. That conveyed everything to Grandma. Hearing about Paru's pregnancy, Grandma wanted to speak to her on the phone. Two days later, she went with her son to a nearby booth and called Paru's home number. She took the phone after her mother-in-law gave it to her. It was unusual for anyone to get a call other than her mother-in-law, but for some business calls from her father-in-law, Paru was very happy to speak to her Grandma.

After pretending for a while, her Grandma asked her, "My darling Paru, when will I see you? I am so anxiously waiting to see my big girl. So you are going to be a mother? That's good news." And she softly added, "Don't you give birth to a selfish boy like your husband. We want Paru, the junior. I will bless you with 10 girls. Many Parus. Oh, I can imagine. Well, Paru, when will you come home?" she said. At this, Paru said, "How can I? You have to get me Koopadi, Grandma. I am waiting. Once I am 5 months old you get me 9 varieties of food with flowers and fruits. I am only three now, Grandma." Grandma stifled a sob and said, "Well, my princess, take heart. I will get you all that you want. My child read good books and a little bit of spiritual books too. If you have a radio or a gramophone, listen to good music. I am happy to hear your happy voice, my precious Paru. My fond love and blessings to you, my child." When she kept the phone, she realized that she had not even inquired about her husband or her in-laws. She told herself, "Who wants to know about the tricksters!"

Paru, the moment she kept the phone, ran into her room and sobbed into her pillow like a baby fighting for milk! She hit her pillow all the time, kicked her sheets and the bed cover, pulled her hair, and, shutting her mouth tight, sobbed. She sobbed and slept off, only to wake up when she heard a loud knocking at her door. She answered from inside, Mayee, "Sorry, Mayee, I slept off. I was near the fire frying the Chikkelunday and so felt tired. I will be there now." Her mother-in-law said, "Alright," and breathing a sigh of relief, she went away. She was only upset that she had to cook lunch. They did not even call her, for they knew the bond between her and her Grandma. Ganapathi told his wife to behave like nothing had happened.

So went that day. When she walked out of her room, Paru saw to it that no trace of her grief was shown to anyone. Only the next day, when the maid came to sweep the floor, she saw the wet pillow kept on the window sill and asked Paru, "Oh, what? Missing your husband? That's a long story. He will never take you to Dubai. Better not cry for him. He is an absurd fellow. God knows how many times he has got ladies pregnant. He would have done it to me, too. The debaucherous fellow." At this, Paru said, "Mind your tongue, woman. One more word, I will see you out of the house. Stop this here and now." The woman said, "Sorry, madam, I only wanted to warn you to take care, madam. You are innocent. Be on your guard." So, what Paru did not expect had happened. She felt the roof had fallen on her head. She just controlled her tears and got on to her normal work. She took her pillow and put it out to dry in the hot sun.

Since she had to be responsible for her unborn child, she decided, "Come what may, I shall face this test of time. If at all Kaveramme and Igguthappa are there, they will protect me."

One day her mother-in-law asked her if she could make another set of baby sweaters and booties in blue. She readily agreed and made it for her. So, on Mahila Samaj Day, her mother-in-law displayed both pink and blue sets for the exhibition. As expected, it won first place, and many women wanted to learn to knit. Paru's mother-in-law, Sarasu, brought two ladies home and asked Paru if she would mind teaching them to knit. "You only have to show them the way I taught you. They were happy to see the two that I knitted and kept for the exhibition. Can you do this?" Paru gave a sympathetic laugh and said, "Yes, Mayee, I will. I love to teach those who want to learn." So, from then on, the Anganwadi teachers started coming home to learn to knit. Paru happily took it as a pastime.

Slowly, she got friendly with them. She got a membership in the local library and started getting books for the 12th standard history group. This became a regular feature. She would study so well and regularly that the teachers brought her the books happily. She was waiting for the 12th exam, but that was far off in May next year. Before that, she will have her baby in December or January. Perfect, she thought.

Things went on. Slowly, everyone at Paru's place knew what had happened. In the beginning, Somu reacted as a brother would, he bombarded and screamed into the phone, and so on. Somu made a sudden visit in spite of his busy schedule on a Saturday early in the morning. He wanted to go and get Paru back home. But his father said, "She is dealing with it perfectly well, my son. Do not disturb her life. We shall think of what could be done once she comes for her confinement. Let us not be rash. Paru is a bold girl. She knows how to react and when." With that advice, he had to get back and wait patiently.

His training, tuition, and commitments hardly gave him any free time, and he worked harder now so as to settle his sister's life.

Since Paru was a sensible girl, she dared not risk her child's life for anything. So she ate well and looked as beautiful as a grown-up lotus. Paru was taught by her Grandma to be an asset wherever she was. In the kitchen, she cooked a good 3 meals a day. At making eats, she knew a couple of them and made them to perfection. She used minimal utensils, and so the maid, in spite of her gossipy nature and getting snubbed by Paru for the same, liked Paru. She only pitied her young mistress. Paru kept a good house. She would ask her mother-in-law if she had made any craftwork or needlework to be displayed. That lady had none. Having come from a fairly well-to-do family, she flaunted her inability to face any strain. But when Paru, her daughter-in-law, worked on tea napkins, table mats, and table covers, she would promptly say she had made them, knowing fully well that her daughter-in-law would never let her down.

It was not in Paru's nature to aspire or ask for compliments. Whenever Paru discussed something in the newspaper with her Mava or her brother-in-law, out of sheer jealousy, Sarasu, her mother-in-law, would call out to her and give her some work, lest they get to know of her intelligence. Nothing disturbed this spirited young girl, brought up by her devoted Grandma. She would give all credit to her Mavi when she wanted it. Her Mavi, when a table covered with a nice design of a basket of flowers was worked on and was completed by Paru she called for a party at home. Some dishes made by Paru were served. Her Mavi brought the tray and, amidst admiring looks at the needlework and eats, declared that she had made them all. All appreciated the work, and unfortunately, her maid came to clear the table.

The guests were discussing the stitches; one said they were lazy-daisy, while the other said they were stem stitches. So, being a prominent member of the Mahila Samaj, she did not want to commit herself. She just said, "Well, well, you keep guessing. I will be back. I can hear some confusion in the kitchen. I hope my daughter-in-law has not burnt her hands while straining tea," and she ran in a hurry. She told Paru to handle the situation. Paru quickly came and said, "Thank God, Mayee came to help me. Now, I will join you in guessing the stitches. Mavi has taught me what is what. Now, these are satin stitches. For the stem, she says stem stitches." This way, she would save her Mayee. But of course, the maid would laugh at the drama and get snubbed as usual. Paru was waiting for her kid to come out to share jokes and laugh.

The fifth month, the month of September, did come. Grandma and mother packed a full-fledged, beautiful meal for Paru and arrived at Paru's father-in-law's place. They had informed Paru's Mavi, so it was not unexpected.

The brother-in-law was also there. Dhanu's sister came with her children. So it was a full house. The maid was engaged for the whole of that day, and so Paru's family was made to believe that Paru had no work at all at any time.

Mother Muthi and Grandma arrived with Koopadi, 9 types of dishes, to bless their Paru. The girl was totally excited. She touched the feet of both of them three times, as is the custom of the Kodavas. They blessed her with a baby without mentioning a girl or boy. All had a nice day, with everyone chatting about home affairs. Machayya Paru's father arrived late as he had some work to do. When tea was served with potato chips and boondi, as usual, Mavi Sarsu claimed that she made them. Paru said nothing. But Grandma knew it all because she was the one who had taught Paru to make the chips differently, scraping on a lined scraper to give them a different look, and also adding a few drops of lime and ginger juice to help digestion! Grandma gave a knowing smile, which Paru acknowledged with a grin.

When Machayya came, Dhanu's brother Karun (Kariappa) served some good brandy, which was appreciated by the men, while bottled juice was served by the maid to the ladies. Later, all enjoyed a heavy meal. What with Neer Dosai, Chicken Curry, Paratha, Potato Palya, Mutton Pulav, Chutney, and pork for those who enjoy. Some rice roti made by Grandma were all packed, especially for Paru, and there was also egg curry, which was Paru's favorite, was it not? The Kesari bath was very tasty, with ground almonds and cardamom. The cashew nuts were perfectly fried with homemade ghee from Pattathi Cow! Oh, so nostalgic! Yet so soothing. Paru ate like never before.

Grandma took her to the side and fed her, tears running down her cheeks. Paru laughed and said, What a teacher! "Don't you know Grandma, you often said, 'Practice what you preach?' Am I to sit and brood here?" "No, my precious, I miss you. You are a brave girl. I will take you to your little cottage in another two months." Grandma said. "I am waiting, Grandma! Then I can be on my own." Said Paru. Grandma found Paru a little too fat for the fifth month. So she asked Paru, "Did you go to the doctor, my girl?" Paru said, why Grandma, I am fine, perfect. Why would I go?" Glaring at her stomach, Grandma said, "I feel you should. I feel you are in for twins! In that case, you need care." "Don't worry, Grandma, I have friends. The Anganwadi teachers, the local hospital sisters—they all come to learn knitting from me. They all said the same. So I am prepared. Anyway, why should I fear when I am going to be with you, my brave Grandma?" She hugged her Grandma and lifted her, at which all screamed, including her Mavi. "No, Paru. Never lift weight." Then Paru begged her Grandma not to tell her in-laws regarding the two-some! With one sentence, Paru conveyed her closeness here!

After lunch, they all had beedas from Moidu-Kaka's shop and sat down to chat. By 3 o'clock, all were tired, and Paru told her maid to serve coffee—filter coffee—for which the decoction was made by Paru earlier. Paru's Thamane (mother's house) folks sipped it with relish and headed back. The Madikeri folks had to fight back their tears once again. Paru bade them farewell happily, waiting for her two little ones!

Months went on. Dhanu would call, as usual, not say a word to Paru. He would speak about his finances, what he had to invest and where, about the gifts each one at home wanted, and about his brother, who was not yet prepared to settle down. This time, as luck would have it when he called unknowingly, Paru took the phone. Hearing a sweet voice from this end, Dhanu said, "Whose is this new voice?"

Paru decided to have fun. She said, "Your good old girlfriend! Have you forgotten me?"

Dhanu said, "I have no girlfriend there."

Paru said, "So you have someone there? Then. I can go my way."

Dhanu said, "Why, who is this? I have never heard your voice before!"

Paru said, "Would you want to befriend me?"

Dhanu said, "Yes, why not?"

Paru said, "But I have thrown you out of my mind long ago. I am Paru, your wife. I hate you and need you no more."

Dhanu was taken aback. "Sorry, Paru, I forgot all about you. How are you? How are you all at home?"

Paru said, "I am fine, and I will not let you be fine. Waiting for you to show you your place."

Dhanu said, "Don't keep the phone! Wait, wait, I have something to tell you." Paru slammed the phone and left the room. The family, which was waiting for his call this weekend, was surprised as to why their son had not called. None of them had the courtesy to even ask him to speak to Paru any time before. What a world Paru had come to, from where, to where!

Paru's studies went on unabated. The Anganwadi teachers and the hospital staff came regularly for their knitting and needlework lessons. That was Paru's only solace. They brought books for her, and she read them with her heart and soul. Now it is November. This month, in all probability, Paru will be going to her father's house, as is the custom. As she was preparing herself, the maid asked Paru, "Akka, what are you getting ready for? Going home? Good. Go and have a nice time. Your people are great to have trained and brought up a child as good as you. Here, the people are selfish. They only think of themselves. You better go there and have your baby."

Paru knew that she was a well-wisher. But sharing home secrets with laborers was not what she had learned. So she told the maid, "Why? When did I say I was unhappy? All are so kind to me. And my husband will get me a lot of gifts when he comes to see his child."

At this, the maid said, "Oh, come on, Akka. I heard you speak to Dhanu Anna. He does not deserve you. He has a keep there. He won't let a female fly past him. You can scold me, but I can only pray for you. After you come, half my work is done by you. I can only thank you."

As she was speaking, Paru pushed her out of her room and locked her door. She kept saying, "Let me clean your room!" and Paru said, "I want to do it myself today. You, please go away." Actually, she allowed the maid to speak because she wanted to know about her husband.

She quickly washed her face and dried her tears. She studied for a while, and then she went to make dinner for the evening. She prepared some egg kajjaya (beaten egg mixed with a little bit of sugar and a little bit of American flour fried in oil) and brought it to the table along with evening tea. When Sarasu, her mother-in-law, pretended that she had made it, father and son passed glances at each other, laughed, and said, "Yes, yes, we know. Who else will cook in the house? Is it not Paru?"

Paru continued the joke and said, "Mayee, your egg kajjayas are nice." Mavi (Sarasu) blushed and went to the kitchen, grateful that her maid had left early that evening. Now the son asked, "What are you making tomorrow, mother?"

She said, "I have to ask Paru what she wants. Poor thing, she'll want to eat something at this stage, isn't it, Paru?" Paru was about to burst into laughter when the doorbell rang. She ran to the door with that excuse.

It was her father. He had come to say that this being the seventh month, they would come, formerly in a week's time, and take Paru for her confinement. During the discussion, Paru's Mavi protested that the hospitals at Gonikoppa were much better than in Paru's hometown and that traveling was hard for Paru at this stage." After a prolonged argument, Machu said that all that was immaterial, that the first confinement had to be at her mother's place, and that he could not disobey his mother, who was too old to take a 'no'. So Paru's Mavi said, "Now that she belongs to Dhanu, I shall speak to him. Let her obey her husband's orders." Paru could take it no more. She only said, "Husband? Don't worry; I have told him. I am going to my Grandma this coming week, and that's final." No one had seen Paru so firm, so vehement, and so confident. She looked like her grandmother when she said so.

So everything was settled. Next Wednesday, Paru's mother and her sister, along with Machu, were to come and take her. Paru got her books ready. She had to return her library books. A little bit of second-term portions had to be learned for after her babies (or baby) came, she would be too busy. Nowadays, coffee is late. Breakfast, many of the times were easy uppittu or nuchi puttu or kadumbuttu. So that morning, she could study for a while and then only come out. Her mother-in-law was surprised at the change. She asked Paru why she was late these days, to which she said, "Anyway, you have to get used to my absence, isn't it, Mayee? So I am giving you some time to get used to the kitchen." Mavi gave her a glare and threw the spoon that was in her hand to the sink and said, "That's not the way to speak to your Mavi." Paru ignored the comment.

Now Paru's Mavi had no way to escape. The very next day, she made a pretense of falling at the doorstep. Then she pretended to have sprained her back. The drama went too far, and she said she had to rest. Their family doctor came to see her and said she was too weak and had to be taken care of. Sarsu started crying, "What will I do with these two men in the house after Paru leaves? Oh, my fate! Should I have become sick now to face all the misery? and so on. Ganapathy (Paru's Mava) was upset, as was his younger son.

Paru our dear innocent Paru was fooled royally! She

never knew that such things could happen. Hers was a practical home; no one cheated, no one pretended. Each one was ready to help the other. Paru thought that this would take a day or two. But this went on and on. The day of Paru's going never came, and soon it was the 8th month. All of Sarsu's friends said, "Never send your daughter-in-law during the 8th month; it's a bad omen." Paru's grandmother also thought so. Now confirmed of the situation Sarsu started moving around. Only she had put on a little more weight sitting and eating, having nourishing food prepared by her daughter-in-law.

This weekend, after hearing from his father that his mother had taken ill, Dhanu said that if he could, he would soon come to see her. The very next week, he came too. He was a little in shock to see a very healthy, plump mother and his well-fed family. Everyone knew that Paru's going was inevitable.

The moment Dhanu came, he pretended to give a hug to his wife after greeting the rest at home. Paru screamed and said, "Don't you dare touch me!" Everyone thought that she was angry because she was not taken along. Dhanu pretended innocence. Then he said, "Knowing that you would not get enough care there, how could I take you? Now, don't get so angry. Let's make up." Paru only gave him a stare. She would not even sit beside him at the tea table.

Now, she thought it was time to act. She called from her home to the phone booth and requested them to call her father. He came and called her back. She said, "Appa, I am coming home now. I do not care about customs, Shastras, or Paddathi. Nothing has helped me so far. If you want me, come and take me tomorrow."

"But my child, tomorrow is Friday, and this is the 8th month."

"Yes, Appa, if you don't come, I'll make a scene; get into a bus and come; or if you say 'no', I will not be seen by any of you anymore." She kept the phone.

Her mother-in-law came in a hurry and said, "What happened, Paru? Who was speaking to you?"

"Don't worry, Mavi; I don't have any boyfriends. I was speaking to my family."

"Oh, you told them that Dhanu had come, is it?" asked Mavi.

She said, "Aah, yes!" and just went to the garden as Dhanu was in the room. She started weeding the flower pots as if nothing had happened.

As expected, that night was hell. Dhanu asked her how she was, and she said, "Who are you to me to tell you ? Should I report to you?" He told her how busy he was and was so happy to see her. She turned back and said," You shameless, debaucherous fool! Do you have the courage to call me your wife? How many women have you got pregnant there? Move away and don't even look at me." Dhanu lost his temper and slapped her on the cheek.

She said, "Thank you, and that's the end. Keep acting until you leave. Or else I will tell everyone what you are up to over there. My brother has found out all about you. We are all educated. We don't care for wealth. Now shut up and keep your distance."

Dhanu pleaded and told her not to tell anyone. She said, "That I will not, for the sake of the ones in my belly. But you keep away."

That was the end of a wrong relationship. Nothing was mentioned outside the room, and everything looked just the same until the taxi arrived with Machaiah and his wife. All were surprised, and protested, Dhanu said, "Let her go and relax. She was quite uneasy last night, and so I called Mava and requested him to take her." Paru just kept quiet. She took the ready box packed 3 days ago and left with no formalities. She did not forget to touch the feet of her Mava and Mayee, and she told her Mava, "Poyith Bappi Mava (I will go and come back)." That was just an assurance to say that she was not splitting the family bonds. A shocked Gappu and Sarsu stared at what was happening, and while the maid gave knowing glances at the pampered elder son, the Dubai contractor returned. The taxi in which Machu had come got everyone totally confused.

Homecoming

A welcome was ready at Machu's place, with a pot of water in front of the house. Mother went in and came out with Arathi and Drishti to drive out evil eyes, and now slowly came someone! Somu was there to greet his sister. Paru screamed and jumped so high that everyone expected a mishap! She had already completed her 9th

month, and anything could happen. Now Grandma scolded everyone and said, "You people behave like babies. What if something had gone wrong?" At this, Somu said, "Ok! That would be my first case." Grandma was happy, but Paru said, "Catch me going to a surgeon instead of a midwife." Dr. Somaiah said, "Oh, my girl, you know all this? And where did you know it from?" "Brother dear, I have been studying for my pre-university. Once I finish, with good marks, I'll go for medicine too," She revealed to her brother regarding the subjects she had taken. Somu said, "Oh, my fate! Once again, I have to see you struggling with your math?" They all laughed, and then, with no questions asked, they all had a good meal. Kadumbutttu (a rice preparation) and Pandi curry (pork). Happily, Paru grabbed the pork dish, and there came Grandma: "No, no, my girl. No pork for my mother in the making'. Here is chicken for you."

It so happened that Baliappa's elder son, Cheeyanna (Chetan), was getting engaged. Somu's Baliappa had come to invite his brother's family, and Somu had come in his car. What a coincidence! He came and joined Somu's family for lunch. He also told them that he would like to take the family Kuthu Bolcha (the standing lamps that belonged to their mother) and keep them with him till his son's wedding was over. To this, the whole family gladly agreed.

After lunch, Paru said that she would rest and went in. The rest of them sat down for a chat. Parvathy's plan was different. She slowly got the 2 lamps from the storeroom and started scrubbing them. She made them shine after taking a lot of trouble and kept them in the hall. She later went away to rest. The after-lunch party went on until the evening, with wedding preparations being planned. All participated. Paru's Baliavva and Muthi, Paru's mom, took an active role in planning the menu. Grandma said pickles were from her, and so also Holige-a preparation like sweet chapatis.

By then, it was 4 PM, and Mother Muthi went to prepare tea for the evening. Paru had a premonition that she would have her baby that night. Slowly, she realized she was right. She quietly caught her Grandma's eye and called her in. In reality, the moment Grandma saw her getting out of the taxi, she thought, "O my girl, thank God you came." Even Somu had a good laugh at her bloated look and swollen face. She looked so pretty, too.

Paru told her Grandma that she was uneasy. Quickly, the midwife was brought in. Thanks to Baliappa, whose car was available at the right time. Seeing Paru, the midwife Savithri said, "Madam, it looks like some complications are there. It's better to go to the hospital." As they were making preparations for the same, Mother noticed the shining lamps. Oh no! Now everyone knew how things had been hastened. It was all because of the strain. Visualizing it could be twins, Grandma came to the hospital all set.

Yes, of course, she had her babies right away—a girl and a boy! The whole night was torture, and the new arrivals came by 5 a.m. on Saturday. The ordeal was over. Mother and Grandma had a hell of a time pacifying Paru. They had to receive beatings and kicks from the otherwise patient sober damsel! It looked like all the pent-up emotions of her in-law's place were gracefully showered on the Thamane folks! Anyhow, all's well that ends well. Paru has been active till the end, attending to her mother-in-law, the kitchen, and so on till the end, and polishing of the huge lamps, to cap it all! No cesarean, no sutures, nothing, and was not Grandma very happy? She now said, "I would have managed it at home itself; why all this hospital and all?" All laughed, saying, "You could hardly bear her ferocious row, and God knows what would have been the outcome if you had tried your prowess. Doctor Grandson came to her rescue and said, "What are you talking about? I am here and would have handled it much better." The family could take the joke no longer, and Machu said, "I did not know that you had training for midwifery. Ok, we accept you as a midwife!" All laughed, and as the joke was heading too far, Somu went to find out when she would be discharged from the hospital. She had to be in the hospital for at least 2 more days.

With the wedding around the corner, Baliappa and Baliavva had to make a move the very next day. Somu shelved all his projects and decided to stay back for 4 more days. Saturday, Sunday, and 2 more days. All arrangements were planned for him after he made a phone call to his doctor in Bangalore. This was indeed an unavoidable situation.

Here, in Paru's in-laws' place, Dhanu (Devaiah) took all his family to task. "Who the hell told her all the nonsense about me? Do you know how she screamed at me?" At this, the younger brother, who was very sympathetic towards Paru, said, "We also heard the slap you gave her.

She is too decent, Anna. Try to make up. Go and see the kids. They are your kids. Let's think of other things later."

Mother bombarded, "How could she scream at my son? Will any wife do such a thing? At least she could have kept quiet." Gappu came to her help and said, "Come on, Sarasu. We all know what is what. What did Parvathy, our daughter-in-law, say when she left? She said I'll go and come back. They are all very decent people. They know to give respect to those who deserve it." The arguments grew cold. Passing a knowing glance at his brother, the younger brother said, "Somu might be having friends in Dubai. At least hereafter, let us learn to shut up Dhanu Anna." Dhanu walked in, saying he did not want his breakfast. Mother fondly called him and fed him his Khara bath and vada from the hotel nearby.

That evening, by 4 PM, all were ready to go to Madikeri to see the twins, Dhanu and Paru. Dhanu was too shy to face Paru. He had one more week of holidays. So he said, "You people go. I'll go on some other day." But Ganapathy would hear none of it. He said, "Either all of us go or none at all. She is your wife. It's your duty to see your children."

At this, meekly Dhanu said, "How are you sure, or how am I sure they are my children? The wicked woman would have had an affair in my absence." His father could no longer tolerate it. He said, "Dhanu, do you want to wash your dirty linen in public? Be quiet. Just say nothing. Let us all go on Sunday. No more arguments." All went to their rooms, realizing how mean they had been to their well-meaning daughter-in-law, in spite of her being the daughter of their own relative.

Dhanu was in a temper, kicking around things, and throwing the newspaper and magazines. Seeing this, his brother quietly entered his room. Things were helter-skelter there. Anil softly called his Anna. "Anna, be calm. Why all this? Now you can only accept the situation. Let us see the babies and come. Patience may result in solutions."

Sunday being a holiday, using his influence, Somu was able to get Paru home on Saturday evening itself, as she was in good health. The moment Paru reached home, she was ready for a deep, good sleep in her favorite bedroom. Mother had arranged for 2 chibbis (cradles made of cane) for the 2 new arrivals. But grandmother would hear none of it. She took them both to her room to enable good rest for the mother. Kids came to Paru's room only at their feeding time. Everything was regularized, and as Grandma packed them tightly and neatly, they would sleep all the time except for change and feeding.

On Sunday evening, Paru's in-laws came to see the new arrivals. Dhanu came boldly and sat down for a chat with his father-in-law. Not knowing anything that had happened clearly, the family behaved like no one knew anything. Only Somu could not even look at their faces. So he went away to his friend's house, lest something untoward happen! He came back only after they left. As luck would have it, Dhanu had left his cooling glasses on the table and had forgotten! So he came back to pick it up. Somu met him at the door. Somu said 'hai' and so did Dhanu. Suddenly, it dawned on Somu that something had to be done. He just told his Bava (brother-in-law), "Bava, I would like to have a word with you." Dhanu said, "Sorry,

I am in a hurry. I have to go to the club."

Somu would take it no more. He said, "I know your life in Dubai, in and out of Bava. Have you married that girl?" Dhanu was flabbergasted at the sudden attack. He said, "What are you speaking about, Somu? Are you joking? I have married your sister Parvathy, as you know. What else, of course, I am married."

Somu blurted it out. "Are you married to the girl in Dubai or not? According to our custom, a married man will not marry again when his wife is alive. So just tell me, are you married to that girl?" "Which girl, what, Somu? What's wrong with you?"

"Bava unfortunately, I will be shifting to Dubai next month on a two-year contract. So I know about all that's happening. I am not forcing you. Tell me if you are married to that lady. If so, give a divorce to my sister. If you don't promise, you will not see her again." Dhanu said, "Well, Somu, I need some time to decide. "How long?" "One month". "No, that is impossible. Give me the answer in 2 days. And this we shall decide before my lawyer.

The shock was too much for Dhanu. He said, "Let me speak to my father, at which Somu shouted, "Did your father permit you to do this horrible act of keeping someone and marrying someone else? Answer me. I have a right to handle my sister's problem."

"I have more rights than you, Somu," said Dhanu.
"Then we shall meet at the court tomorrow. Come with your lawyer."

Once again, Dhanu was speechless. He said, "Give me 2 days' time, and I'll tell you what I have decided."
"No! I want you to tell me tomorrow before noon. I'll be in Gonikoppa, at the Kamath Hotel. We shall finalize or I'll meet you at the station, I mean the police station."

Dhanu regretted his oversight and forgetfulness and walked off. That night, the family of Gappu saw Dhanu very disturbed. Everyone knew that he was at fault. His father told him, "Look, son, he has given you an option. Just tell him and give up that woman. With that, the road is clear."

His brother said, "Yes, Anna, better late than never. Now that you are married, forget the past. Then you can take Paru Mamma to Dubai and be happy."

Dhanu was apprehensive. "Oh, she will boss over me. I don't like to be bossed by anyone. You know it. I don't want to be a henpecked husband. I am a Kodava after all!" Father rose from his seat and said, "You did not remember all this when you indulged in wrong activities, and now you became a Kodava? I order you; if you want to remain my son, give up this dirty game."

Dhanu was a daredevil. But today, all his courage failed. He knew that of all the property his father had, only 10 acres were ancestral. The rest of the 60 acres were self-acquired. His brother started in his own jovial way: "Anna, don't give her up, Anna; then I'll be a rich man with all of Appa's property. You will have 5 acres of ancestral land, and I will have 5 from there too."

Dhanu got so angry. His mother came to save him. "Why, he can do what he wants. A wife has to adjust, doesn't it? Why should she question her husband? Her role is to serve him."

Gappu Ganapathy got very angry. He said, "Look, Sarasu, this sort of unwarranted, misplaced sympathy and love made him a spoilt boy. You are the root cause of his getting spoiled. Now allow him to correct himself. He is 29 years old. Let him make his decision. He will have me or that woman, whom we don't know. Choose my son. If you want your father, delete her from your life."So, saying, Gappu just collapsed on the chair. That must have been a mild heart attack. The family doctor came and treated him and said, "Please do not give him any tension."

During their visit to Madikeri last week, Gappu's family hardly saw Paru or the kids. They were so confused that when Paru said, "How are you, Mava, and how is your leg, Mavi?" they could hardly answer. The 2 brothers only saw the babies and left, or did their eyes see the babies at all? Mavi Sarasu came near Paru and said, "Rest well and come, my daughter-in-law. Take care of our babies, our vamshakudi. Paru smiled.

By the way, all the arrangements between Somu and Dhanu were unplanned, and no one in the family knew of it. Paru did not even have the time to talk. But the eyes of the brother and sister spoke. When she saw Somu, she knew what had happened. Seeing Paru, he only said, "I will sort it out for you, my sister." With all this tension, that night Paru developed a slight fever. With a little bit of medication from her brother, she recovered too. So all at home said, "Kalla pani," only a "pretended fever" to get the attention of her brother!

The next day was hectic for Dhanu and Somu. They met at the Kamath Hotel in order to avoid the family. Matters were more or less settled. Dhanu assured Somu that when he came to Dubai, he would see a changed person in his Bava. And that was that. In 2 days, after assuring his father that things would be settled, Dhanu left for Dubai.

Somu and his family had 2 happy days with a full family, like the good old days. It was tough for Somu to see Paru lying down all the while. On the third day, which was Tuesday, in spite of protests from Grandma, Somu made Paru walk a little. Paru realized that she wasn't sick after all. This time, when Baliappa came, he installed a black-and-white TV in his brother's house. Cricket matches were just being relayed. The family sat down to watch, Paru lounging on a grandpa's easy chair. Thanks to Baliappa wanting the Kuthu Bolcha (the standing lamps), which in fact hastened Paru's ordeal, and thanks to Paru's painstaking polishing, Somu was there to see his little niece and nephew.

Grandma was particular to declare that the girl came first, and so she was 'Akka'! Just imagine that among twins, one is a senior! Grandma was so busy, and so was Ma Muthi. What with bitter medicines, bathing Paru, and bathing the 2 little ones. Now, Machu decided that unless someone was engaged in all this, he would have to face sick people at home all the time. So Gangamma, a regular maid, was hired. An expert at these tasks for bathing Paru and the babies. But yet, Grandma and Mother made it a point to be with the babies all the while, giving instructions meanwhile.

When Somu left, he said he would miss the 2 dolls. The little ones were so small that one could hardly figure out their features or who they resembled. Yet, in Machu's house, everyone saw in the girl a resemblance to Paru and the boy to Somu. Somu said to his Grandma, "You better make them bigger for the naming ceremony at least." Grandma only said, "Don't cast your evil eyes on them. They will fall ill. You go away. Do not stare at them." and so on. Somu left with the satisfaction that he was there at the crucial hour. But no one knew what happened between Dhanu and Somu that Sunday.

XIII

Dr. Somaiah in Dubai

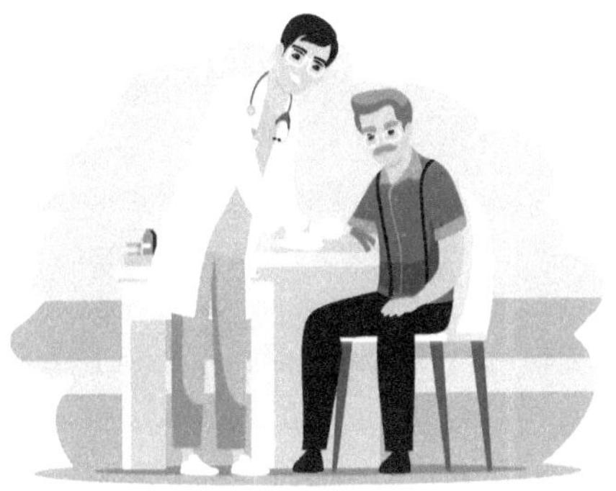

There was never any proposal for young Somu to go to Dubai. But that day, he decided he would. The idea was not taken well by his family. But for the sake of Parvathy, they were all prepared to take the chance. A Dubai-based company welcomed Dr. Somaiah with a very handsome salary. He could also come to India once a month. It was a contract of 15 days there and the other 15 days of the month in India.

Somu's plan was perfect. When Somu went to Dubai, he was very happy at his job. But it took him quite a while to get in touch with Dhanu. Dhanu tried his best not to meet him. In a month's time, making friends with some big-wigs there, he found out Dhanu's whereabouts. He did not tell Paru what his plans were.

In the little town of Kadagadala, Dr. Somaiah rented out a good building to start his nursing home. The family by now had shifted to Kadagadala as the weather in Madikeri became too oppressive for Grandma, who protested strongly for this plan. In spite of that, Grandma had to agree, as all the others liked the change. The fields in Madikeri would be taken care of by Machu. Now he had bought a bike too. The little fellow got his rides now and then, whenever he visited his avvaya and big avvaya. He was Cariappa (Kavan), and his twin sister was Kamavva (Kanya). They were now four years old, and both were mischievous to the core. It was not an easy task to manage the 2 brats whenever they came home.

After the children, Paru did not sleep over her plans. She completed her BA degree course and took a B.Ed. side by side. So, she started teaching at a school in Gonikoppal in spite of protests from her in-laws. She sent both the kids to a nearby play home and brought them back when she returned from school. So no burden was given to her, Mavi, who did not like too much work. Fortunately, her brother-in-law took to the children fondly, and both the kids were on his back all the while.

Dr. Somu's nursing home started in earnest and Grandma thanked him for keeping his word. One day he told his Grandma, "It was all because of your grandson-in-law. I went to Dubai only to save my sister. There, I really struck a good deal." Grandma was now keen to know what happened. He told her the whole story.

Dhanu was a spoiled child from his childhood. Naughty at school, bad at studies, quarrelsome, disobedient, and so on. His brother was good enough, but a pleasure lover. Ganapathi doted on his daughter and got her married to a wealthy planter, who had his parents here in Kodag. Her husband was a Major in the army. She had 3 kids; the last of them was a boy. He was now in the 10th standard. So she was not able to come to see her brother's twins.

Once, when she had planned so well, her husband was posted to the border, and she had to be in Delhi. That was a very tense period. Her younger brother went and stayed with her for a while because the situation was tense. The army had lost track of him, and she had to pretend as if nothing happened so as not to worry her parents. Her younger brother held the fort and maintained secrecy. This year, after her son's 10th exams, she was to come to Kodag. The elder one was of marriageable age, and the other was in his second year of engineering. They were all going to come down sometime now. The whole family, including Paru and the kids, were planning a good time.

Paru had knitted beautiful sweaters for the 2 sisters, which suited the cold weather of Delhi. For Paru's son, Paru's husband had brought a nice bicycle. Mavi was busy with the goldsmith, getting some good jewelry for her daughter. As they were on their way, Kami's family heard from Major Gappu's son-in-law. He was to come after a week and was coming for a long holiday. Kamavva, or Kami, as she was called, knew nothing about the confusion that took place between Paru and Dhanu. Since Dhanu was to come only by the end of the month, the family planned a trip to Thala Kavery when both men came.

Kami first went to her mother-in-law's place. Kami had lost her father-in-law long ago, soon after her marriage. Her younger brother-in-law squandered a lot of his father's wealth. The elder one was a bank employee, a very straightforward officer, working in Virajpet.

As is the way with all Kodava families, Kami first came to her mother-in-law's house from the train. She was fetched by her younger brother-in-law, who was always at loggerheads with his mother. Kami's mother-in-law was so happy to see the two girls, who had both become so pretty and good-natured like their parents. When they did their prayer to the hanging lamp (Thook Bolcha) in the hall (nellakki nadubade), they sang 'Adikaveramme Devida Padakekolu Mangalam'.

This made their Grandma very happy. But she was not so healthy, and so too much work made her tired. The girls were not happy when they were asked to keep their things in order and help their paternal Grandma. There used to be regular fights between the younger son of Kami and the Grandma (Kami's mother-in-law). Grandma would lose her temper with her daughter-in-law. In just a week's time, Kami said, "Mavi, with your health, too much disturbance may not be good for you. I will go to my mother for a while and then come to you after some days when my husband comes." Her Mavi, though she pretended to protest, easily agreed to this proposal. Poor thing, what could she do with her bad health, one son who did nothing but pick up quarrels now and then, and another a regular bank employee?

After a week with her Mavi, Kami headed to her (Thamane) mother's house. Her younger brother-in-law brought her there. He was very fond of the girls, too. He dropped her off at her mother's place. He had a drink or two with Gappu (Kami's father), and he said, "Let them be here for some time. Where will they get so much peace in our house? Avva is always screaming her top off." Gappu only laughed. Kami giggled and said, "It's ok, Bava; it's getting late. You better leave soon. Otherwise, you are in for trouble." He smiled and left. Kami laughed and told her family, "He is so notorious that he gives endless worry to Mavi. Poor Mavi. At least she has patience with him. I wonder what my mother would have done." Everyone laughed because only the 'Wearer knows where the shoe pinches'. Paru quickly got busy with the girls. They were pretty darlings, and the elder one was daintier than the younger one. Little Kanya took to Kannika, the elder one of Kami, the moment she saw her.

Talks were going on regarding Kannika's marriage. Kannika did not bother with the discussion at all. She was sure that she did not want to marry anyone on the estate. Having stayed in the city all through, she wanted someone in the city. Offers did come from some planters, some army men, some working in government offices, and some in good companies. Her first question was, "Will he let me work?" The officers, having come from well-to-do families, were not sure and left. This time she told her mami (Paru), "Look, why are they in a hurry to get me married? What will I do at home after marriage? Rear children?"

Paru asked her, "If you don't mind, can you tell me what your qualification is?" She said, "I only did my B.A., and since I did not score well, good colleges would not give me seats. So I told them that I would go for B.Ed. Ma says, "Where is the need?" They have kept me at home for a year and are waiting for me to agree to a marriage to which I will not agree unless I stand on my feet. So many of my friends have gotten married and are caught in the rigmarole of life. I hate to be one of them." Paru told her how she could study further privately. But she said she hated studying. Paru was surprised. "Then what shall we do? We will find a solution. I will talk to my friends."

Kannika found a good friend in her Paru mami and said that she never thought she would find a friend in this regard. When Paru went in to make some tea and 'vade' for the family. Kannika said that she hated cooking. Paru laughed and asked her if she liked reading storybooks, to which she answered in the negative. When Paru went to arrange the bedrooms for the night, Kannika said she hated dust and would get sick if she dusted or was there when the bed was being made. The vases were beautifully arranged with flowers and ferns from Paru's home garden. Kannika asked whom she hired to arrange the vase. "Of course, it's my house, and I'll arrange." "Oh, I hate vase arrangements." "Well, what do you like, my princess?" said Paru, patting her on her pretty cheeks. She promptly said, "Watching TV." "Go ahead, my girl; enjoy your holidays. See you later," she said, and she went in to prepare supper.

The cook did not know how to make rice ottis, so she asked the cook to make some mutton curry and started kneading rice otti. Young Padma came along. She said she would love to learn to make ottis. So Paru taught her to start with small balls patted into small shapes, and she taught her to roll the ottis. Oh, what a mess Padma made! Both of them laughed and played, spreading the rice powder all over the kitchen. The maid who was making the curry said, "Now, now, if madam comes, you will both be whacked on your backs." The laughter and screaming made the mother and daughter come in.

Mavi Sarsu said, "Oh my God, what has happened to you both? Look, Kami, is this what you have taught your daughter?" Kami only said, "Clear it up before someone slips and falls." Together, they completed the ottis, while the maid cleaned the kitchen. Sarasu was quite patient with Paru after the bad incident at home. She knew that Paru could love a devil because of her generous outlook.

When all these things were happening at Gappu's place, the little ones, Kavan and Kanya, were absent because Anil, their Cheriappa (brother of Dhanu), had taken them out to the park. It was their usual practice to send the children to the park. If they did not play, they would refuse to eat. Today, returning from the park, Kanya came home with a small scar on her knee. She complained that she fell down, and she cried aloud. Kavan cried louder than her and kept saying, "Akka Akka boo, blood." So now it was Paru who had to attend to them and bathe them, lest they sleep off without eating.

Bathing was no joke, for the slightest burning sensation would make the two scream, and later, after bathing, they wanted to speak to their big avva at Kadagadal and convey their agony. Big avva (Paru's Grandma) spoke to Paru and said, "If you can't take care of them, send them here. You are too busy with your guests and have neglected my darlings," and so on. Paru felt like laughing, but the kids kept sobbing to attract their big avva. Now the budding engineer, the younger daughter of Kami, took over and told the kids that otti prepared by her was ready and they could eat. Paru took them to the nellakki nadubade, the central room of a Kodava house, made them say their prayers, and then Padma began to feed them. Rice otti and mutton curry. One or two pieces they ate with relish. Then they started rolling their food in their mouths. Both pretended to throw up.

The little naughties always played their trick and avoided eating. Paru came with the usual thin bamboo stick (Thoore kolu) and just made a noise on the table. Quickly, both said, "Not me; it was she; it was he!" and tried to eat. Both begged Padma to feed them with honey and ghee. They were both happy. Regularly, calcium tablets were being given to them, as Dr. Somu said they had to have. Both, as usual, took it and left the dining table, and of course, they dumped it in the dustbin. That was the usual. After brushing, they went to sleep with their Cheriappa, who told them stories.

That day, as his nieces, sister, and nephew were all around, he told the kids that he was tired and so they had to sleep without a story. Both pretended to be asleep. After Cheriappa left their room, they took the soap and made thick soap water, and started playing in the bathroom. In a while, Paru came to see what they were up to as she heard them laugh. The scene was miserable. They had put soap on the bathroom floor, and both were busy playing a sliding game. They had soap all over them. They were a sight for the sore eyes! So, the thoorekolu came out again. With due apologies to their mother and another washup, they went to sleep. Both were so naughty that Sarasu Mavi was often reminded of her two sons when they were young.

Two days later, both Dr. Somaiah and Dhanu Devaiah came from Dubai. Oh, now it was gifts galore. All had lots of gifts, perfumes, and radios with batteries and handbags, dry fruits and dolls, small cars, and what not! When Somu Mama left that evening, the twins wanted to go with him to Kadagadal. Just before starting, they opted to stay back. Poor little ones. They wanted to stay as well as go!

Paru's people were invited for lunch that weekend after Kami's husband came. He had purposely worn his uniform. When he came to show off to the little ones, young Kavan Cariappa declared that he would become General Cariappa and so wanted an army dress. Their tailor there got the material and stitched it in two days.

What a time they all had that day! Only Grandma was very tired after the journey. Dr. Somu's car was a small one; the sun was too much on Grandma, and so was the fatigue. By evening, they had all dispersed. Little Kavan stuck to his father (Dhanu) all the time and told him he would love to go to Dubai with him. The little girl felt strange to be near him and so stuck to Padma, the engineer in the making.

Kanika, who at first only wanted to watch TV, has now started joining Paru in her work. Paru told her how 'an idle brain is a devil's workshop'. She told her the stories of the great women of India and how Bharathmatha needed useful women. Kanika, with her advice, tried to go through her B.Ed. books and said they did not interest her. Later, she took an interest in nurse training. So she decided to join the nurse's training course once she went back to Delhi.

The twins loved their Cheriappa Charmana (Chiru),and he was their favorite of all in Gappu's house. He was not thinking of marriage at all. But nowadays he was often coming home late. When asked forcibly, he said that he was in love with a lecturer. She was a Christian girl. There were a lot of objections. It was not easily accepted. But finally, they had to, lest the younger brother follow the elder Dhanu. This once again agonized Gappu, a staunch Kodava and a person always after some good project for Kodag and his people.

This time, Dhanu had come on a long holiday. He decided to spend some time with his father, who often fell ill these days due to heart trouble. He also wanted to spend some time with his children.

Now Paru, who was working as well as being the pillar of the family, took the courage to ask Dhanu, "My husband, is there any chance of my joining you in Dubai?" He had some excuse and said that his house was being built there, and once it was ready, they could all be together. Paru carefully asked him, "There is not much of a relationship between us, as you and I know. Can you at least tell me what is going on? Did I come to this house as your wife or as a manager? I will have your answer this time." Dhanu said, "Now now, do not rake up old problems. Now that things are settled, why are you digging up the old?" Paru said, "Children are growing up. They should know the situation. Whether there are only two children of yours or more of them, I do not want someone else to tell them. Do you only have two children or more?".

Dhanu suddenly raised his hand to slap her. She caught his hand and said, "I am now a different person. These threats don't scare me, nor do I want to disturb my father-in-law's health. But here and now, I want an answer: When do I come to Dubai, or when are you coming back to settle in India?" He said, "Let us discuss this later," to which she said, "Don't make me pick up a row. Tell me the truth, and let's face reality. Be sure that I will not leave this family. I may be able to be without you, but not without this family. I will be true to my in-laws."

Dhanu left the room in a huff. Paru decided that things had to be settled at some stage. So she called her brother and told him to fix up a day to talk about it. A meeting was fixed in two days' time. Only Somu, Paru, and Dhanu met at a hotel in Gonikoppa. Paru said that she would accept his terms, and he had to accept hers. She wanted the truth to be told. Somu was waiting for this day. He wanted his sister to speak up and stand up for herself like a bold Kodavathi lady.

Dhanu said finally, "Look, Paru, I have a wife in Dubai. I have a child too, a baby girl. She is just a year older than my twins. Coming to Dubai will make things worse for you. Children will not understand what is what. My job there depended on that relationship, and so on. "So you wanted a housekeeper to take care of your parents. That I have understood. But I want this to be told to your parents, and I want a share of your property. I do not want to put my children in trouble in the long run. I do not care about what happens to you. But I do care for my in-laws, who have been kind to the wife of a debaucherous husband. And these things will be settled before a lawyer," said Somu. "Oh, why all this, Somu? Let's just be the way we are. Anyway, there is not much between us. Paru is too strong a woman to be an obedient wife. So let things be as they are."

Somu said, "Look, Bava, I have certain responsibilities as a brother. Now, when Chiru gets married, it will not be the same. They are all, unlike you, very nice to my sister. But I can't leave her in a dilemma. It's time I got married too, and so we have to settle this matter this time." He said, "Please not this time. Dr. Somu. I have to speak to my father-in-law in Dubai." Somu said, "Nothing is going to wait, my dear brother-in-law. I will take legal action against you if you try to escape this time.

I have not troubled you so far, despite knowing all your foul play. Paru knows about it too. I was waiting for her to raise the issue. This should have been settled four or five years ago. But things took different turns. Paru's babies, Gappu Mava's health, and so on. It's high time now. If you really want your Mava's permission from Dubai, ask him to come. Now the ball is in your court. Take the challenge and finish it."

Dhanu had no alternative, and so they departed, proposing to meet in a day or two for decisions with the lawyer at Gappu's house.

XIV

In Bangalore

Baliappa's son, Advocate Cheeyanna (Chethan), who got married four years ago, did not have any children. His wife, Lalitha (Lali), was also an advocate. She had, from the beginning, wanted to practice. Both being busy, they had shelved having children for a while. This had caused no end of worry for Baliappa, Baliavva, and their family. Aiyanna and his wife, too, were concerned. But Cheeyanna and his wife were lawyers. Who could argue with them and win? So time had just gone on. Finally, when they did decide to have their child, they found that they were not successful.

Offerings to various gods failed to bear any fruit. In this connection, there was unpleasantness in the house. Balliavva cursed her fate by calling her a barren woman. She was sorry for her son. This was certainly expected, as human frustration can make one inhuman! When things were getting worse, Cheeyanna spoke to his mother and then to Paru's father, Machu. Both of them tried to convince him that it might happen later. But the doctor, a famous gynecologist in Bangalore, said that it was a bad case. Plans were going on for an implant, which was not Grandma's choice. Finally, that also failed to bear results.

Those days, Bangalore had orphanages from which getting to adopt a baby was not so difficult. When they wanted a boy, Chiru's wife said a girl would be her first choice. So a 6-month-old baby was brought home. It took some time for Lali to love the child. Grandma had to stay in Bangalore, in spite of her age, to teach Lali to love the child. The baby, who was not loved by anyone at the very outset, was now slowly being accepted. Father Cheeyanna Chethan could never take to her. The little girl became Grandma's pet. She would call her 'Avva' which pleased Grandma immensely. She, the little child who was called Chintana, would often ask each one, "Do you like me?" That was very pathetic for her, Avva, and she would, with her shaky hands, plait her hair and say, "You are the most adorable child I have ever seen."

Chinthana was now two years old. Nowadays, she was

a part of the house. She knew that something was not alright. She was bold enough to ask her father, "Appa, am I not your favorite? How about a fond kiss? I'll give you five kisse s in exchange. Will you give me one Appa?" Slowly Chetan started realizing his mistake. He told his wife, "Don't you think it's unfair for us to tease the poor child? In case we had not taken her, some good soul would have taken her and given her a good life." Lali now agreed. Yet it took some time to realize that they could not hurt someone for no fault of anyone.

Grandma Chinthan's 'avva' was now in Kadagadal. It was Chintana's third birthday. Paru's twins were 7 years old. They all came to Bangalore in a taxi. Machu, Muthi, Grandma, Paru, kids, and the party went very well. That was when, after dodging for so many years, Dhanu was pulled up by the family. The youngsters arranged for a party at a restaurant. 'No elders, please' they said. More than anything else, they did not want emotions to mar the health of the seniors. Well, the twins were happy with Grandma and their cousins, with the ladies serving them snacks. Paru said she missed her Mava and Mavi. She apologized that her Mava's health did not permit him to come.

Little Chintana had grown so cute, and she looked gorgeous in her many new dresses, everyone said she almost resembled Lalitha, which made Lalitha happy and made her get closer to her. Chintana asked her mom, "Amma, do you love me as much as big Thayee loves me?" Lalitha was so taken aback, realizing that the child had visualized something. She promised herself that she would love her Chintana sincerely hereafter. Big Thayee

(Grandma) fondled her and told Chinthana, "No one can love you as much as your mom." Chithana was the star of the day.

Paru was a little worried regarding the outcome of the youngster's meet. But her sister-in-law said, "Oh! My husband would never let a split take place, and Lalitha assured her that even advocate Cheeyanna had never split any family.

The men came back quite late, by which time dinner was ready. After dinner, Paru's brother called her and said, "He has agreed to certain conditions; you should put up with some too. One cannot change the dictates of the Lord. Any rebellion would cause ill-feeling, splitting, and agony for the twins." Paru was sure she would put up with anything if told by her brother and her cousins.

The outcome of the discussion was not very promising for Paru. She had to put up with the wife of Dhanu in Dubai and her only daughter. Dhanu promised that she would never visit him in India. He also told them that she would not need anything in the property as her father was a millionaire and had three daughters only, each having a bungalow to live in and an apartment each in their name. Paru agreed to everything, and Dhanu and Paru decided to live like husband and wife before their elders but had nothing to do with each other. So the children were safe, and that evening the Kodag folks left on a late-night drive back home.

In the car, many things were discussed as the two little brats got into their Appa's car along with their Cheriappa.

The family planned a trip to Delhi as soon as Kami, Dhanu's sister's husband, had a month's vacation. Kami had not been able to attend the birthday party of little Chintana.

Paru, on her way back, had lots to share with her brother, parents, and Grandma. She wept bitterly as never before. While the discussion was going on, Grandma said, "My little Paru, life is like that. A woman is born to bear many onslaughts in life. All will not be like Rama: 'eka vachana eka bana eka pathni vrithastha'. "Yes, Grandma, my fond gannoo. I don't want Rama, who distrusted his Seetha."

They had a short break for tea, and then Dhanu's car crossed them. The sleepy little ones screamed, "Race them, Appa. Amma! We won! We won!" Grandma told Paru, "Treat what has come to your share as nectar. Other people have worse situations." She also said that if an old soul like herself was around, she would not even have allowed the freedom she got with Ganapathi and Sarsu. That she was allowed to work was the highlight of her life, and that was true. She is now taking her Master's degree exam in May, after which she will be a lecturer. She promised her Grandma that she would never leave her in-laws and go away in search of better pastures.

Unfortunately, that night Grandma took ill. She used to fall ill now and then these days and would get admitted to the nursing home. But this time, she was pretty bad. She was in the hospital for a week or more. Paru had to take leave to take care of her. She, Grandma, was ninety years old now, and no one wanted to celebrate her 90th birthday for fear of evil eyes. She got well and came back home, and their favorite maid, Kempi, was engaged to take care of her. Machu's brother from Bangalore came down to stay with his mother along with his wife. His sons were too busy. The trip to Delhi was in the offing. After Paru returned, her husband declared that the trip would be by the end of the month. So preparations were afoot. Information was given to the Delhi folks. Kami and the girls were so excited. The young brother of theirs, Biddappa (Biddi), was very anxious to see his little friends. Major Chengappa (Chang), as he was called, was busy planning the itinerary. He planned a trip to Kullu Manali, a hill station in Himachal Pradesh, which is about 2050 meters above sea level. As the guests were there in Delhi for a fortnight or less, the trip had to be short. Paru's parents, her in-laws, and Kami's parents were all here. So the four-bedroom house was rather full, and so Paru's parents-in-law and her parents were made comfortable in the nearby apartment of a friend of Major Chengappa, who had gone to England for a holiday to visit his sister's family. His quarters were within walking distance, which was good as the oldies could rest now and then.

When they left Kodag, Grandma assured them that she would not neglect her health, for negligence on her part meant that the family holiday would be disturbed. No need to say that the kids were happy to stay in Delhi along with Padma and Biddu. They had their own plans. Little Chintana was their main attraction. Padma had engaged an ayah to attend to the children and a cook too. When the trip was planned for Kullu Manali, Sarasu and Gappu refused to join them. They were too scared, as Gappu had already suffered two mild heart attacks. They said the trip to Delhi was good enough for them, and so a taxi was arranged to take them around Delhi. Padma had seen Manali with her engineering students, and Biddu's preparatory exams were just over, and he had to prepare for his CET. So he, too, stayed back. Kannika was happy to go along with Paru. So, the team was Paru, her parents, her husband, her brother Somu, her husband's brother, and his wife (the newly married wife Lilli). The group headed for their trip with warm clothing, proper shoes, raincoats, and so on.

Of course, the children protested that they too wanted raincoats, shoes, and so on. But seeing Padma and Biddu not going and Chintana also not interested, they said it was OK to not go and needed no raincoats.

XV

A Family Trip

Manali was colder than expected. When the flight took off, they could not make out. Later on, the AC became intolerable. The clouds had gathered so dense that it was scary, and this was only the second time Paru had sat on the plane. The flight to Delhi was not so scary, but this height made her feel awe-struck. For just a show, Paru had sat near Dhanu. Suddenly, she screamed and hugged him tight. The younger lot glanced and behaved like nothing had happened, and Somu gave a knowing smile. Dhanu soothed her, patting her head. Realizing what had happened, Paru suddenly straightened herself and tried to be on her guard. Dhanu liked the change, and now he knew that they were not enemies after all.

Reaching Manali, the hotel rooms were booked. The hotel keeper greeted them and directed them to the four rooms. One for Machu and his wife, one for Kami, Kannika, and Paru, and the other for Somu Dhanu and Chengappa. In the end, it was for Lilly and her husband. Though Kami missed her Chang, she was the host and had to stay with the ladies as her daughter had no company. So Paru was to be with her along with Kami.

That evening, they made it to Rohtang tunnel. Stepping out of the room, all of them saw how beautiful the scenery was. 'It is like Madikeri on a higher hilltop,' they said. The lush green forests, the swaying winds, the chill weather—it was like heaven on earth. They walked around in the park for a while till their turn came for their trip to Rohtang Pass. Oh, it was scary. The sound of the mountain winds was awe-inspiring. It was about 3000 meters above mean sea level. Chang told them how the soldiers had fought in those areas during Chinese aggression. There were no facilities, and people would take 21 days to carry food to the soldiers on head loads, braving bad weather and enemy threats. Then they saw museums depicting Himachal culture. Their guide told them that this pass was the connecting pass to Kullu.

The next day, they visited Hidimba Devi Temple and Siyali Mahadev Temple. The architecture on the pillars, the wooden cutting, the half moon, and the lotus petals were so realistic. The structures of Gomatha, the Naga and Ishwar temples, and the massive doors with bewildering engineering skills were all so enormous, they thought. The couples were together all the time and, in fact, had forgotten about the beauty of the architecture. The temple bells attracted Paru a lot, and she jumped to strike them, and Dhanu carried her up to reach them! Things were patching up, making everyone happy.

The next day, first they visited a Buddhist temple nearby to perform some pooja. When the couples came together, the holy man there blessed everyone and blessed Somu and Kannika together, and both of them blushed scarlet. Then they headed off, shopping. Manali has a long range of shopping malls. It is traffic-free, so walking around with no care was easy. They went to the Dungri village market. Shawls and sweaters there were as soft as silk. They could be held in your fist. Shopkeeper, there was a very nice man coaxing everyone to buy more. Stoles were of varied colors. The men were all busy purchasing gifts for their wives, and Somu did not fail to buy one for Kannika! The shopkeeper there ran around this group, seeing the purchasing spree of these tourists. They could bargain like nobody's business. Paru and Kannika did have a nice time buying things for the ones who did not come.

Now, all were hungry, even though they kept eating this and that now and then. They sat down to hog in a Japanese Mizutaki (eatery). They ate sushi, a special fish. They had lovely momos, soups, noodles, Okafu, tofu, and so on. Paru, in her notebook, noted down the names of the dishes. She had also noted down the places she visited.

They took pictures in parks, temples, and shopping centers. In the evening, they visited Vedavyas temple.

Dog-tired, they all came back to the hotel where they stayed and, after a wash, ordered a proper meal, where they could hardly eat anything. The men had some Japanese drinks, and the ladies tried wine. Kannika told them that their mother, Kami, had some good homemade wine at home. Paru said, "How secretive you are, Kami mamma. Is that all only for army folks?" She said, "No! I have plans of serving it with grilled chicken and cutlets once we are back in Delhi." "Well, well, I am looking forward to learning from you, mama dear."

That night itself, it started snowing. It was unusual for Manali to have snowfall at that time. But the Major said that no one can predict the weather. "The earlier we start, the better it is, or else we will be struck here." However much they tried the flight, which was to be by noon, was shifted to 8 p.m. Both Paru and Kannika were happy, as were Lilly and her husband. They all went out in the snow and played with snowballs, throwing them at each other. They made a snowman like kids do and tied a ribbon around his neck. Kannika's shoe got stuck in the snow. She was unable to walk without it. Paru and Lilly had to be helped by their husbands. It was inevitable for Somu to carry Kannika back to the rooms. That was a filmy scene indeed. Haha, like Rajkapoor walking with Nutan! Blushing all the time, both enjoyed the mishap.

They had to finally get ready in a hurry to reach the flight on time. Thank heavens, the flight took off by 8 p.m. as scheduled. As the weather prediction was known to

Padma, and with information given to her by her father, she did not panic. There were Gappu and Sarsu, who had to be pacified. When the team came, in the early hours of the morning, Gappu and Sarsu were still at Chang and Kami's place, all the time worried. Only after a breakfast of Idli Sambar from the hotel did they all retire to their respective rooms to be woken up at 11 a.m. by the little ones. Now they had only four days to go. One day was for a party with Chang's army friends.

The next day was sightseeing in Delhi. One day's rest, packing, and back home. The hosts said a tearful farewell to the departing party. Kannika sobbed unusually. Somu felt sad too. With his eyes, he wished her well and said they would soon meet. They quickly departed, and Chang wished Paru and Dhanu all the best and said, "Life is only adjustment, dear brother! If you do, you are the winner, and if you don't, it's your problem." Dhanu thanked him for everything, wished his brother-in-law and Kami, wished the girls, and said knowingly to Kannika, "Let us hope to meet soon."

The Bangalore and Kodag gangs got into the same flight as they were to part only in Bangalore. Kanya was all excited to board the plane, and so were the twins. But the trip to Delhi, the gifts, the parks, all the excitement made them so sleepy that before the plane moved, the little army succumbed to the hugs and kisses of the sleep fairy!

XVI

Grandma, The Fountain of Love

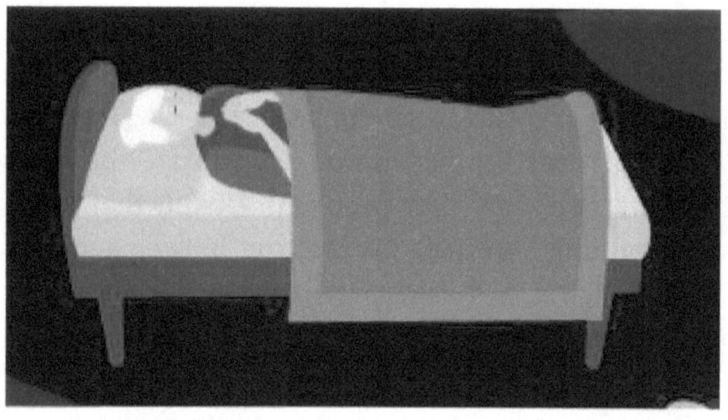

An untoward mishap awaited the family. A message had already reached Somu that Grandma had suffered a massive heart attack. The doctor at the nursing home had saved her from the sure end, and so the cars without stopping in Bangalore charged to Kadagadal. Grandma, who was in her old house at Madikeri with her elder son and daughter-in-law, had to be rushed to the nursing home of Somu, which he had called "Sanjeevini," as suggested by his Grandma. Sanjeevini rejuvenated

Grandma, and she beautifully responded to the treatment. By the time the party arrived, Grandma was all smiles.

Now she told her Somu that she would not go without wishing them all after all! Somu now decided that he would see that she totally recovered. Gappu and Sarsu came to Gonikoppal as soon as they heard the news. The Bangalore grandchildren were planning to leave the next day for Gonikoppal. But Kanya said, "Another day with big avva, please." No one could refuse her plea, as Grandma also hugged her so tight that the twins said, "How about a picture with Grand Avva and the 3 of us!"

Sathar studio was very famous in Madikeri those days. Sathar was called for a photo session. Sons, daughters, and mothers; Grandma and grandchildren; and many combinations of photos were clicked. One was an individual photo of Grandma, on her request. Everyone teased her and said, "Oh, our beautiful Grandma, you are still young and want an individual photo," and all laughed to their heart's content.

They all retired, and that was when a phone call from Kami woke them up. In their confusion, they forgot to tell Kami what had happened here.

When she came to know, she was so angry. The whole lot of them charged to Madikeri to see Grandma by the next train and reached her as soon as they could.

At Grandma's behest, a heavy lunch was arranged the next day. Grandma that day called Kannika and asked her if she would like to be Somu's life partner. She ran away, blushing. When Somu was asked, Somu eagerly agreed. The rest of the family knew it all! Grandma said that it was a mini-engagement party. She made them both stand before the Thook Bolcha, the hanging lamp in the hall, and all at home blessed them.

Grandma was very happy because, the moment she saw Kannika, she knew that She was meant for her, Somu. Matches are made in heaven, aren't they? And it so happened that it was Grandma's birthday. In fact, Grandma didn't even know her birthday. Somu and Paru had fixed up the date of June 19th as her birthday. Every year both of them would celebrate it in their own way, Grandma's birthday. Today was the 19th of June. Grandma had a pair of bangles, which she had worn as a girl, in her cupboard. Often, they would go to the bank and come back for emergencies. She asked Paru to get it. Paru brought it and said, "Ah, Grandma! For me? How sweet!" Grandma snatched it off her and said, "No, my naughty. Today is Kannika's day. This pair is for Kannika; this is a nose ring of mine; I am giving it to Somu. He has to get a ring made with it." So the gifts were given, and there was a lot of fun too. Somu gave the lovely shawl he had got for his Grandma from Manali, a soft Pashmina shawl in a powder pink shade.

Everyone wished Grandma a Happy Birthday, and they made the children burst their balloons, which were filled with colored paper pieces. That day was a lot of fun, as Paru's mom Muthi had also baked a nice chocolate cake, the recipe for which was from Dhanu's gift book of recipes for her sometime back. Grandma requested her son Machu to get her Pathak and she asked him to tie it to Muthi's neck as she was too tired to do so. All were so happy as Paru slowly came and told her Grandma that she and Dhanu were happy with each other. Hearing this the old ebbing-out Grandma gave a happy satisfied smile and said, Jaya Jaya, shred Krishna. It was a perfect birthday and a befitting engagement too.

The little imps had their food, and leaving them with Grand Avva and Kempi, the seniors went for their dinner. As dinner was getting over, Grandma coughed a little. Somu came running and said, "We will shift her to the nursing home." Grandma begged him not to do so and said she would surely agree to do so the next day. She called Muthi and asked her to get the key to her chest. She took out her favorite double chain and two sovereigns. She gave the two sovereigns to her two daughters-in-law and gave the double chain to Paru. Doing so, she hugged all her grandchildren, and slowly, her breathing became frail, and she breathed her last!

That was the end of Grandma. The house was crushed with grief, for they never knew how it would be without the iron lady! Adieus and farewells were beyond the reach of the family. The beautiful soul traveled peacefully to the unknown destination.

The pillar of Paru and Somu's home had bid goodbye to them. It was tough to face. But the brave lady had left behind a bunch of brave people; they knew not to be crushed under grief. They had no clue as to how to lose a battle. Grandma's family were winners, even in distress!

Epilogue

Today, Paru is forty-five. Brother Somu is in the U.S. His nursing home, Sanjeevini, is getting maximum attention in Kodag, with specialists visiting the nursing home as and when required. Somu comes once or twice a year and spends a month or two. Somu's Belliappa is no more. He died due to negligence. He had neglected his liver problem without revealing it to anyone. Sarasu and Gappu are happy in Gonikoppal, and Lilly (though a Christian) is a very nice person. She takes care of them, and so, leaving her responsibility, Paru can often come and stay with her parents. The twins—one is helping his thatha on the estate, and the girl is doing her medicine and is in her final year.

Kannika has completed a course in occupational therapy in the U.S. and is a great support to Somu, who has to be here and there. Chintana has grown and become an artist and a good singer who sings for films. She is even now the apple of everybody's eye. Lilly's two boys are at Bishop Cottons in Bangalore, and both are very good hockey players. One is going for his Air Force selection soon.

Padma, Kannika's sister, has decided not to marry. As luck would have it, Somu and Kanniaka had a child who had a heart problem. He had heart surgery at the age of three. Thanks to the care taken by Somu and Kannika. Padma, Kannika's sister, is such a support to them.

Gappu, Paru's father-in-law, is now unable to go to his estate, and Paru's son takes care of the property. Machu's brother Somu's Baliappa, is no more, as already mentioned. His son, who is quite efficient, does his best, though the younger one squanders a lot.

Now is the time for Paru to dream of her past. Those days she would sit on her self-made swing, tied up in the cattle shed, swinging high up in the air, and play. Now she imagines herself going into the sky and reaching the stars. In her dreams, she goes floating and suddenly wakes up to reality.

Paru was always a strong girl. She would hardly fall ill. Sometimes she would pretend to have a stomach or headache and lie down. But she could never lie to her Grandma. The moment she saw her Grandma, she would burst into fits of laughter.

One day, as she was returning from school, a cyclist dashed against her, and he lost his balance. Paru fell down. She was not very young, as she was in V standard. Her brother went to hit the cyclist. Paru pretended to have fainted. They had to carry her home on his bicycle. After coming home after a while, she behaved alright. Complaining of headaches and body aches. She was not sent to school the next day. No homework either. Her Grandma said, "What a weak girl you are. For a small knock, should you become so sick?" She could no longer control herself, and her Grandma and she had a good laugh at the drama.

Once, she fell into the lake while collecting soft mud to make craft items. She really lost her balance. At that time, when she screamed, no one went to help her, not even Somu, for they all thought she was pretending.

Paru thinks of her pranks with her Grandma. She would climb up the Guava tree and pretend not to be able to come down. When Somu would run to help her, she would jump down and say, "You are fooled!"

Nowadays, Dhanu goes to Dubai only once in 2 or 3 years. His father-in-law in Dubai passed away, leaving his daughters with enormous wealth. The Dubai wife has taken to one of his secretaries and is not keen on Dhanu. So, only to see his children, he goes to Dubai once in a while. He does not want them to come to India only because he does not want to disturb his family. They are good children and love their father. They do not approve of the nature of their mother and so do not want to be a burden to their father, as they have enough wealth in their names.

Paru barely speaks about the past, so also her in-laws. 'Past is past' she thinks. Sarsu now keeps herself busy attending to her husband. Now and again, he falls so sick that he is on a wheelchair. Though a busy bee, as usual, Paru always has time to dream. She has a vegetable garden and a lot of flower pots at Gonikoppa. In her absence, her mother-in-law takes care of it with the help of her gardener. Gappu walks slowly between the plants and says Paru made our lives worth living, to which Sarasu agrees.

Paru's father, though old, never feels so. Machu still has a small axe in his hand. He attends to Paru's garden in her absence. He remembers his good old days with his mother and the way he met Muthi when he had gone for a festival at Kakotuparambu. Muthi looked just like Paru, he tells Paru. Whenever Muthi makes Chakkuli, a fried eatable, he says," It's not as nice as the ones you gave me in your house when I came to see you". Paru and Somu, together, even now pull the legs of the old couple. Machu gets brinjal, and whenever Muthi makes ennegai and rice otti, he says it's not as nice as the first meal you served me after coming to my house, and she says, "Oh, that was in Madikeri house. Now we are in Kadagadal. Here, the taste of brinjal is not so good." and all enjoy the fun.

Life goes on. Paru will be a Grandma too. Somu will come back and settle in his nursing home. Kannika will be a good wife. She was also Grandma's selection and Grandma can't be wrong!

Glossary

1. **Imara:** The wooden seat seen in ancestral Kodava houses
2. **Achu Nayaka:** One of the well-known leaders of Kodag
3. **Igguthappa:** One of the deities worshipped by the communities in Kodag where they pray for rain
4. **Thula bhaara:** An offering made to Igguthappa by way of a balancing scale. The person sits on one side of the balance, An equal weight of rice/jaggery/coconuts is offered to the Lord
5. **Kokkethathi, Jomaale, pavalasara and Pathak:** names of Kodava jewellery
6. **Okka:** Family in Kodava language
7. **Karonas:** Ancestors in Kodava language
8. **Kattole:** Threshold made of wood, that separates two rooms.
9. **Mahila Samaja:** Ladies club
10. **Kaveramme:** a deity worshipped by the people of Kodag
11. **Kajjaya:** A fried sweetmeat, made of rice and jaggary
12. **Uppittu:** A savoury dish made of semolina
13. **Nuchi puttu:** A savoury dish made of broken rice
14. **Kadumbuttu:** a Kodava dish prepared with broken rice, made into small balls
15. **Pandi curry:** A pork delicacy eaten along with Kadumbuttu
16. **Kuthubolcha:** Tall vertical lamps made of brass
17. **Holige:** A sweetmeat made of dal, coconut and jaggary
18. **Khara bath:** A breakfast dish prepared out of semolina
19. **Bava:** Brother-in-law
20. **Mamma:** Sister-in-law
21. **Thalacavery:** The birthplace of River Cauvery
22. **Nellakki nadubade:** The central hall in the ancestral house with a hanging lamp, where prayers are carried out
23. **Thoore kol:** Bamboo stick

About The Author

Monnanda Shobha Subbaiah, the second daughter of Biddanda Aiyappa and Poovamma just stepped into the octogenarian world!

She had always taken a keen interest in literature and art. She pursued various art forms with the encouragement of her parents and the teaching facilities available at her hometown. She studied at the Central High School and later at St. Joseph's Convent, Mercara. After completing her Bachelor's there, she proceeded to Manasagangotri, University of Mysore for her Master's program in Philosophy.

She married Monnanda Subbaiah, Executive Engineer PWD, and traveled to different parts of Karnataka along with him.

She pursued her interests in literature and art through her journey. She founded the Lion Ladies auxiliary at Kushalnagar, immersed herself in social work, nudged ladies of the district to find their voice and participate in community activities. For her social service, she was awarded The Best Social Worker i.e., Rajya Puraskar in the year 2001. She instituted Mysore Sangeetha Nrithyakala Sabha, a Dance and Music school with support from her husband, and contributed to the field of Art. She conducted a bespoke State-level Dance competition where the winners were given visibility at prestigious events across the state. She became the deputy commissioner of Guides in Kodagu for 8 years and earned laurels. After the demise of her husband, she launched a kindergarten Vee Kids which she named after her him whom she fondly called 'Vee' (for Victory), and ran this institute for 25 years.

Following are some of the accolades she received:

The title *Nruthyakala Sindhuri (1996)* in *Mysore:*
The *Sangeethothsava Prashasthi* by the *Kannada and Culture department (2010)* in *Mysore*

Invited to present programs on Art and literature on *Doordarshan National television*, of which her Kodava-related programs (*Narimangala, Bhaaratha Vachana of Jaya Bharatha*) are popular. She has composed and rendered them with her team of singers who are part of her family. Her *Akashavani* programs on Music, Chintana, Dramas, and Stories are popular.

She was chosen as the *Samelana Adyakshe of Kannada Sahithya Parishat (2018).* She received the *Karnataka Kodava Gaurava Sahithya Prashasthi in 2022 and 2023.* She has written 8 books in Kannada, and 8 in Kodava language, of which, 2 books each written in Kannada and Kodava language have won awards. These books include poems, short stories, life histories, epics, and translations.

In 2023, she received the Fellowship from *Karnataka Kodava Sahithya Academy* for her extensive research on *The Culture and Tradition of Kodavas,* written in English. She continues to write and publish her books, articles, and journals and richly contributes to society.